THE LONG-KEPT SECRET

ENTER THE WORLD OF ROMANCE

ALEXANDRA LAMOUR

authorHOUSE

AuthorHouse™
1663 Liberty Drive
Bloomington, IN 47403
www.authorhouse.com
Phone: 833-262-8899

© 2023 Alexandra Lamour. All rights reserved.

*No part of this book may be reproduced, stored in a retrieval system, or
transmitted by any means without the written permission of the author.*

Published by AuthorHouse 10/17/2023

ISBN: 979-8-8230-1592-9 (sc)
ISBN: 979-8-8230-1591-2 (hc)
ISBN: 979-8-8230-1590-5 (e)

Library of Congress Control Number: 2023919237

Print information available on the last page.

*Any people depicted in stock imagery provided by Getty Images are models,
and such images are being used for illustrative purposes only.
Certain stock imagery © Getty Images.*

This book is printed on acid-free paper.

*Because of the dynamic nature of the Internet, any web addresses or links contained in
this book may have changed since publication and may no longer be valid. The views
expressed in this work are solely those of the author and do not necessarily reflect the
views of the publisher, and the publisher hereby disclaims any responsibility for them.*

Prologue

1847

Elizabeth lay in bed, tossing and turning her head from restlessness and pain, while the stout nurse tried to relieve some of her discomforts by placing a moist, cool cloth upon her perspired forehead. Elizabeth prayed that the child would be born soon. Again, she screamed in pain until her final screams became a baby's frantic cry for the first breath of air.

"Is it a boy?" she implored with bewildered blue eyes gazing and fixed upon the nurse's red face.

"No, Lady Montgomery," the stout midwife responded as she stood over the circular silver basin. "It is a beautiful girl."

The nurse passed the baby to her assistant and then sat by Elizabeth's bed. She watched the stern midwife work with great prudence as she cleansed the baby before wrapping her in fine white silk linens made for a princess or a child of great affluence.

A horse's gait became audible and louder as a tall man with fair hair and round brown eyes dismounted his horse with expedience.

"Open the bedroom doors," Elizabeth requested. "My husband has arrived."

She happily looked up to see Lord Montgomery standing at the doorway. His robust body and debonair appearance still moved her deeply. He had the power to lure any woman into a world of dreams and fantasies. As always, she knew that business in the North had almost caused him to miss such a joyous occasion.

"Oh, Jonathan, I thought something had happened to you …"

Lord Montgomery, ecstatic with emotion, approached her and touched her colorless lips to preserve her from overexertion. "I'm here," he said.

She felt comforted by his loving words.

"Elizabeth," Lord Montgomery said while carrying his daughter in his loving arms, whispering words into her ear. "We must give her a name." He turned to look out the window and thought for some time until his eyes caught sight of the pinkish-to-purplish flowers in the vase. "How about Fuchsia? Yes, Fuchsia," he repeated, highly pleased with the name he had chosen, and laid her back into the cradle by their bed. Then he turned to his wife, who had already fallen asleep, and to the stout nurse who gazed up at him with great reverence and a pleasant smile.

He returned a smile that confirmed that her conscientious toil had not been in vain, and he walked out of the room. Before closing the doors, he glanced back at his wife and the baby's cradle.

Lord Montgomery went into the library and poured himself a glass of brandy. One of his favorite rituals was to drink alone while everyone slept. It gave him time to reflect upon concerns that were troubling his mind. Pacing the floor for a while, he walked over to his desk to retrieve a cigar. Glancing at the painting of his wife triggered his fickle emotions. During their month long stay in New York, he had met an upcoming artist, Blake Carrington, who had painted his wife's portrait shortly before their move to Charleston. She wore her favorite blue dress, which he had bought her in New York, with hair, dark as the night, entwined into a long tight braid that hung past her right shoulder. She was not beautiful, but she was elegant. Her perfect poise and speech could easily charm any man.

He had important matters to ponder concerning his daughter's future. He wanted Fuchsia to have the best of everything, and he was confident she would. It would be necessary to send for Miss Hathaway, one of the best teachers from London, according to his mother. Lord Montgomery had always believed in a vital education. Being an Oxford graduate constrained him to encourage education for both sexes, often resulting in inevitable disputes among his peers. He believed a woman should be able to conduct herself with flawless social grace and intellect.

Miss Hathaway's arrival made him realize he had made the best choice for his daughter's education. Over time, he believed Fuchsia loved her deeply because she catered to her child-rearing and academic needs much more than her mother who was preoccupied with social gatherings and household duties.

After the first two years of marriage, Lord Montgomery's discontent with his wife's lack of affection and attention grew. They used to dine together every evening, which altered to once a week. Furthermore, instead of being fun and playful with plenty to talk about, the heavy quiet as they ate and strain for conversation slowly revealed the weakening of their relationship. Time had revealed the truth of a relationship that lacked the strength to withstand life's changes. As a result, Lord Montgomery's wandering eye inevitably led to a torrid affair with a staff member.

Finally, at half past two in the morning, he arrived at his bedroom, undressed, and waited for Priscilla, an African American household servant. She was a dazzling eighteen-year-old woman with the most charming, radiant smile that made all his troubles disappear. She had a slender body, large brown eyes, and wavy black hair, which was only let down at night after her daily chores. Her light brown skin was soft and silky, and it blended with her hazel eyes. Her perfect waistline was the envy of every worker, and she enjoyed teasing the others by wearing a tight corset that emphasized her full, round breasts.

"Priscilla," he whispered as he closed the door quietly behind her. "I have a little gift for you."

She dashed to his side, her eyes widening with glee. It was another jeweled gift, one more to add to the collection he knew she hid in a velvet case under her mattress. He had concealed the intensity of his love for her, and he knew she did everything to please him by endeavoring to fulfill his every need.

"Thank you. It's beautiful," she responded.

With eyes of admiration he reached for Priscilla, affectionately kissed her cheek, and whispered, "I love you."

It had been several months since their relationship developed, and he yearned to share his feelings for her. He wanted to tell her how much he loved her, but he knew it would stir up matters, forcing her to leave the plantation for good. He tried to tell her she meant everything to him, but he remained silent and gave her one of his loving glances. Their liaison became known one day when Priscilla announced secretly to her sister Georgette that she was with child.

PART I

Chapter 1

1861

As Fuchsia rode over the rich, sumptuous fields, her black and wavy long hair blew in the wind. She approached the workers as though to speak, but she rode by them with swiftness, kicking her heels against the horse's sides to pick up more speed. She had just turned fourteen. Her physical appearance made her look much older since her body was firm and relatively mature.

Horseback riding was best, in her opinion, in the late afternoon since it gave her a sensation of freedom and pleasure. She loved the sun's descent and its brilliant colors illuminating the sky with its grandeur and glory. It was, without a doubt, the most enjoyable time of the day in her eyes, and she always shared it alone. Unfortunately, on this particular day, there had been talk of a civil war close at hand, and she feared it greatly. However, riding helped her forget about her worries.

It was one of the hottest days ever in Charleston, South Carolina, especially for field workers who began at the crack of dawn and continued until the sun set on the scorching red horizon, foreshadowing another unbearable day ahead. When the great bell that stood visible on top of the barn rang, sighs of relief would appear on their dark, stern faces as they stopped another day of rigorous toil. She gazed over the vast tobacco fields toward the sunset while the last stacks of tobacco were placed on the carts. She always sympathized with the field workers, especially at the end of the day as the wearisome, slow procession of men, women, and children approached the barn.

It was another humid evening like it had been for the past week. A faint breeze formed and lingered in the air, giving Fuchsia a carefree feeling as she rode passionately toward the prodigious manor. She adored the seasonal flowers that gave off a sweet and pleasing aroma, a unique quality to South Carolina. The white colonial marble columns at the main entrance gave her a feeling of family pride. Its unique structures were common in the South. Such craftsmanship demanded patience and incredible skills, according to her father.

In the parlor, her mother sat with her hands folded on her lap as talkative women conversed in circles about daily gossip. One pleasant neighbor, Mrs. Fitzpatrick, glanced at Fuchsia, inviting her to join in when she saw her at the doorway.

In the library, Lord Montgomery's profound conversation took place with his close friend, Lord Wellington. Montgomery's hair, slightly whitened along the sides and back, gave him an aristocratic appearance. He continued chuckling as Wellington demonstrated various movements with his hands and body, seeking to make their conversation even more humorous.

Fuchsia leaned against the wall beside the library door and listened intently to the gentlemen's conversation.

"Well, my friend." He chuckled and slapped Lord Wellington's back.

"I must disagree with you. The Northerners are asking for too much. Say, John, my boy, there is talk that war is imminent. President Lincoln said that we better prepare ourselves for it." He leaned closer and sipped his brandy.

"I loathe the very thought of it, but man will never cease to amaze me. He has to learn the hard way, and then it's too late," McDuff

The Long-Kept Secret

added with a serious voice and a Scottish accent. He puffed on his cigar as though he didn't have a worry in the world.

Fuchsia had heard enough. Fear filled her heart as she headed to her bedroom. She undressed and went immediately to bed, dismissing the intense conversation of war that she had overheard in the library. She tried to convince herself it was just talk.

Later in the evening, she awoke to someone's voice in the hall. She detected furtive whispers. She could not hear their words, but the more they spoke, the more curious she became.

Fuchsia got out of bed and leaned against the door, attempting to listen, but there was dead silence. She went to the open window and fanned herself because the heat was unbearable. As she was about to return to bed, the moonlight revealed someone in the fields. The person was making discreet movements and turning around periodically. Fuchsia distinguished that it was Georgette. She immediately recognized the housemaid's bulky body and unique limp from a birth defect.

Fuchsia dressed, put on a light shawl, and went out into the bleak night. Suddenly, rain started pouring upon the earth, making it muddy and annoying to walk on.

"Georgette!" Fuchsia raced toward Georgette, hoping she could hear her cries in the torrential rainfall. When she reached her, she said, "I saw you from my window, and I couldn't understand where you were going, especially at this time of night."

"You better hurry up, my dear, or you'll catch a cold. You are always so curious about my whereabouts. As a child, you followed me almost everywhere."

They returned home and dried off in the hallway.

Flowers wrapped tightly in a sack slipped from Georgette's grasp.

"Flowers? Why would you be carrying flowers under your cloak?" Fuchsia asked.

Lady Montgomery's distinct footsteps sounded in the main hallway. The echoing of her footsteps ceased, and she stared at the two women. "Go to bed, Fuchsia!"

3

Fuchsia rushed out of the room without saying a word, knowing that her mother would deal with her the next day. As she climbed the revolving staircase, the brass-framed mirror vibrated slightly from the abrupt closing of the library door.

After Georgette changed her clothing, Lady Montgomery asked her to join her in the library.

Georgette entered reluctantly.

Lady Montgomery walked to the window and sat on a tall chair with embroidery on the seat. Her blue eyes were blazing. "Georgette, she must never find out, do you understand? It is our secret, and no one must ever know about it."

"Yes, ma'am," she responded.

Lady Montgomery rose from the chair, picked up the sack of flowers, and wiped the moisture from her hands. She walked over to the mantel, pressed them against her slender figure, and cried softly to herself.

The next morning, Fuchsia sat in the library alone. She straightened her long skirts and strived to perfect her appearance for Miss Hathaway. Her tutor prepared for her return to London. Since the war was close at hand, Lord Montgomery had encouraged her to leave immediately. She had been Fuchsia's dedicated instructor for most of her life, spending inspirational afternoons at the Charleston library.

A week after Miss Hathaway's departure, it was indeed war! The Southern attack on Fort Sumter at Charleston on April 12, 1861, began the Civil War. Lord Montgomery had decided they would flee to England that night for refuge. Horses were stationed and packed in the stable. He had deliberately hidden most of their fortune in a chest beneath the earth, hoping they would return home when the war had terminated.

The Montgomery household was in upheaval as Lady Montgomery and the servants prepared to leave as soon as possible, fearful of the

The Long-Kept Secret

lurking danger. Lady Montgomery worked hard packing whatever things she could get her hands on until Lord Montgomery appeared at the bedroom doorway, stunned.

"Where is she, Jonathan?" cried Lady Montgomery, walking to the window and grasping the curtain in her trembling hand. "They have taken my baby; they have taken her from us."

"I'm here, my dear," he responded, unable to remain calm.

Elizabeth fainted on the wooden floor.

He tried to revive his wife, moving her on the bed and gently slapping her cheeks. "Elizabeth, wake up. We must leave now."

By the time Georgette had brought a bowl of water and a cloth, Elizabeth had regained consciousness. She gazed around the room, opening and closing her eyes. Lord Montgomery's words of consolation reassured her that they would find Fuchsia soon.

Smoke suddenly penetrated the house.

Georgette's screams from the hallway revealed that grave danger was close. "Fire! Dear Lord! Fire! It's everywhere! Lord Montgomery, what we gonna do?"

"Save yourself, Georgette," he said.

She raced to their sides, confused and terrified, and helped Elizabeth to her feet while choking frantically for air. She darted to the window and tried to open it. Her attempts were in vain, and she fell to the floor, unconsciously.

Lord Montgomery lost consciousness and released his wife's hand.

The oxygen in the room was sucked out, and the fire enveloped the house within minutes. Everything in the room—wooden table, bed, embroidered chairs, and curtains—burst into flames.

The leader of the group questioned the whereabouts of the owners and learned they had perished. Outside, fearless soldiers filled with greed and enmity believed the war was for a noble cause. A couple

5

of surviving servants—disoriented, exhausted, and covered in ash—surrendered to the Northerners.

Fuchsia reached the top of a small hill that gave a perfect view of her home. The wandering had finally ended. With a surprising dismount, she pushed back her hair and rubbed her hand against her mouth with trembling fingers over her lips. Her majestic home was no longer standing! The war had obliterated everything except for the barn that stood amazingly in almost perfect condition. The animals had probably been stolen along with much of the grain, soil, and tools. She stammered out words of confusion and swallowed. Her throat was dry. A feeling of suffocation overcame her. All hope crushed, she walked along the barn, feeling no reason to live.

Simultaneously, she fell to the earth with uncontrollable screams and stopped to catch her breath, whispering that it was only a horrible dream. Fuchsia tried to compete with the truth, but it was too conspicuous to believe anything else. The remnants of her parents' and Georgette's clothing were spotted close by, but she did not possess the strength to examine what was left of their bodies. She vomited at the sight and fell to the ground. How was she going to face the reality that she possessed nothing? She was truly alone. Her life looked gloomy beyond belief.

After some time of grief, a new kind of energy soared through Fuchsia's body. She visualized her parents and Georgette telling her to be strong and to have faith. Drying the tears from her eyes, she looked to the heavens and prayed to God for help. She prayed that everything would be as it had been someday—perhaps even better. *One day at a time,* she thought. *I've got to hold on. I can't give up!* Her life had miraculously been spared because she was riding the day her family was taken from her.

Fuchsia shaded her eyes with her hand and looked about; she had spent the night in the barn with some straw as a mattress.

The Long-Kept Secret

Mr. Jones, an old neighbor, approached her, which caused a sudden fright. "Fuchsia is that you? I'm so sorry about what happened to your home. I'm in the same mess."

He had survived after the burning down of his cabin and wandered over to the Montgomery plantation for help. The old man had dark circles beneath his eyes and partially opened lips as he asked for water.

She walked over to the well and found some near the bottom. By the time she returned, he was sitting upright, looking at her with compassion and complacency. He was a kind neighbor.

"Drink this and rest a bit," she said. "You can lie down in the barn if you wish."

"Thank you, my dear," he responded, happy to have found a place to sleep and someone compassionate.

Fuchsia had never experienced such insurmountable grief. She knew it would take a long time to heal from the pain. Her eyes swelled with tears again, and she hopelessly tried to force them back. The burned heap of waste before her was intolerable. Fuchsia caught sight of a few unscorched pots and pans that the flames had spared. Her father had prepared his family for tragedy, and he had trained her frequently on what to do. She had to work diligently since the soldiers could reappear on her property.

After locating the manor's front doors, she counted the steps, walking over the wreckage and the rubble toward the buried chest that possessed the family's fortune. Finally, she reached the most critical step. "It is here!" Her integrity exploded in her, reviving positive emotions that had dominated the past. She fell to her knees with a scorched spade.

Mr. Jones assisted Fuchsia and dropped from exhaustion, striving to regain his breath.

"Take a break," she said. "I can do it myself."

Mr. Jones left and reappeared with a long metal spoon. "I think this will help."

She alternated the spade with the spoon until she heard a clang. Her face lit up with hope as she tugged on a metal chest that was one

Alexandra Lamour

foot wide and two feet long. It was heavy and required them both to lift it out of the earth. Some of her anguish vanished. She knew there was enough money to cover her basic needs, the reconstruction of the home, and paying employees to run the plantation. The plantation was all she knew from childhood. It was part of her being, and her family had sacrificed to keep it operating when the tobacco fields lost money due to stiff competition from neighboring growers. She was the essence of everything it represented, and Fuchsia knew it had to be rebuilt.

The plantation was vacant of soldiers. The barn would be an adequate temporary shelter from the night and weather. Fuchsia lay on a pile of hay, wiped her tears, and wondered why God had allowed such a calamity to enter her life. And why had He taken three of the most significant people from her, especially when they were all she had and probably would ever have? She lacked sleep, and her stomach ached for food. She decided to try to sleep and forget her present situation. Then she whispered, "Once the war is over, life will be better."

Chapter 2

Life in the orphanage was difficult before the war and even more so during it. Suzanna Smith, a beautiful young and dynamic girl, had turned ten when the Civil War began. She had been at the Charleston orphanage from birth. The scarcity of food and water forced the orphans to seek their own survival needs.

Mrs. Ryan, an elderly lady, managed the orphanage for several years. She had grown weary since she suffered from different illnesses, including a chronic cough caused by emphysema. Heavy smoking over the years had taken a toll on her lungs. Her lack of care for all the other children put them in the most deplorable situations. Also, money was scarce since donations had stopped when the war broke out.

Suzanna and her friend Mary searched for food in the streets in the early evenings. Stores were rarely open to serve customers since the streets were dangerous with looting and shootings. The men of Charleston fought tenaciously for their land and lives. The thought of Northerners taking over their land was inconceivable.

One particular store owned by Mr. and Mrs. Owens gave leftovers to Suzanna and Mary at nightfall. Also, they gave them canned foods whenever they were available. Canned foods were like gold, preserving food for lengthy periods. They were kind-hearted even though they had lost two sons during the war.

Alexandra Lamour

Suzanna was the leader of the group and did her best to make sure the orphans had basic needs. She was also a dreamer. She hoped one day she would find a family to enjoy the luxuries of a safe and nurturing home environment.

At night, she would lay awake wondering about life outside of the orphanage. Her mind drifted to enchanting places filled with beauty and mystery. Far away lands that she had read about at the Charleston library. Her favorite story was Charles Perrault's classic called *Cinderella*. It was about a young maiden whose beauty and charm captivated the heart of a charming prince.

Her hope of finding such a man never diminished.

Chapter 3

Fuchsia received happy news from a young soldier on horseback one afternoon. Long-anticipated news had arrived after four treacherous years and had spread across the South like a whirlwind. The news would alter a generation and the generations to come forever. Robert E. Lee's surrender to Ulysses S. Grant at the Appomattox Court House on April 9, 1865, verified the abolition of slavery, which spurred the rapid growth of American industries. It was a time to rebuild and restore the damages that left thousands homeless, hungry, and disconsolate.

Unfortunately, there was too much to do at the plantation. First, she had to go into Charleston to find laborers, which she knew wouldn't be difficult since so many people were looking for work; young, old, male, and female would be willing to take on almost any occupation to get back on their feet.

The following day, she asked a soldier heading into the city to give her a ride if it wasn't troublesome. As they rode into the city, she was amazed by the incalculable amount of people rushing as fast as their legs could carry them. Several buildings were under reconstruction.

One of the stores on the corner of Pine Street, *Lawson's Mercantile*, caught Fuchsia's eye. She immediately dismounted the horse and thanked the young soldier. Then she noticed the small sign over the main door written in black print: "If We Don't Carry It, No One Will."

Alexandra Lamour

After she entered the store, a middle-aged man with a shaven face approached her joyfully, half laughing and smiling, until the sound of a cannon exploded, leaving Fuchsia voiceless. First, the man reassured her that there was nothing to worry about since laborers were expanding Pine Street by knocking down some hazardous condemned buildings. Then, his mood altered as he harped about the Yankees taking over the city of Charleston like it was their own.

After several moments of trying to regain her composure, she spoke. "I'm looking for some strong men to assist in reconstructing my home." She cast inquisitive glances around the store.

"I'll be back in a minute," he replied.

She coughed several times from sawdust in the air. There appeared to be no order in the store; there were several kinds of tools, different sizes of nails, a basket of fresh vegetables, and piles of wood stacked against the wall. She could not identify the remnants of materials sloppily piled on the floor and walked past them.

The man returned with three children: two brothers, aged ten and twelve, and a young lady of fourteen.

"Many orphans are looking for work; the two young boys lost their parents in the war. The young lady has been orphaned her entire life. The orphanage brings them to my store to help me periodically."

The orphans looked at Fuchsia.

He said, "I'm sorry no one else here could provide better service, but everyone is too busy rebuilding what they have lost." He placed a finger on his forehead. "If you continue down Pine Street, you'll come to the unemployment building. I'm sure you'll find more than enough help there."

"Thank you," she answered and noticed the girl smiling. "What is your name?"

"Suzanna Smith."

Fuchsia glanced at this vision of loveliness. Suzanna's remarkable beauty touched Fuchsia. Her fair curls were neatly combed to the sides and fell past her shoulders, not quite reaching her waist, with gleaming streaks of gold. "You are pretty." Fuchsia thanked the man

The Long-Kept Secret

for his time and made a hasty exit, feeling guilty for leaving the needy orphans behind.

She was thrilled to discover how many people would work for her. She bought several carts, a couple of wagons, fresh and canned foods, tools, supplies, extra clothing, and magazines containing architectural designs for homes. She purchased seeds for the garden she had already begun and a few samples of textile fabrics for the draperies. She thanked God wholeheartedly as she led a few workers back to the plantation.

To her surprise, when she arrived, Suzanna was talking vivaciously to another employee. Their conversation terminated as she approached.

"I see you have found my home, Suzanna."

Suzanna's fiery eyes became somber. "Oh, please, ma'am! Tell me I can stay with you. I don't eat much, and I swear I'll be a hard worker."

Fuchsia favored her immediately. She got out of the wagon. Then she placed her hand on Suzanna's shoulder. The orphan shook from nervousness. She released her grip, walked over to the cart, and selected the best apple in the basket for Suzanna.

Mr. Jones rapidly approached them. He was choking for air. "The chest is gone!"

Fuchsia rushed toward the trees where she had hidden it and saw a woman mounting a horse. With Suzanna at her side, they mounted a nearby cart and raced through the scattered shrubbery and trees at full tilt. Fuchsia grabbed her arm as they rode side by side. The stranger pushed her with such force that Fuchsia fell to the ground. She remarked the thief proudly looked back at her with victory on her face.

Fuchsia remounted the wagon and snapped the whip against the horses' backs. They charged toward Charleston.

When they entered the lively city, people were rushing along the streets. Just as they turned a corner, nearly crashing into another cart, a young boy beckoned them with a stick, hollering over the racket. They descended and approached him.

13

Alexandra Lamour

"I know who you want. I saw the thief myself. Miss, I'll tell you where she lives if you reward me."

"Speak, child!" Fuchsia exclaimed. "You'll be rewarded plenty, but you must tell us the truth!"

The young boy appeared to be dallying with them, which caused Fuchsia to become impatient. He held out his hand for money and then pointed to the floor above the unrestored store that stood out among the other newly rebuilt buildings. With an impetuous ascension up the stairway, they reached the top level. Then they noticed one door with light flowing through its cracks.

"It has to be this one," Suzanna whispered as she turned the handle on the door.

The woman had her back to them and was gazing out of the window. The chest was on the bed with the money sprawled out, and the thief had neatly piled gold and silver coins and many bills on the table.

The woman turned in alarm.

Fuchsia said, "Did you think you could outwit us?"

Suzanna flicked the whip in her hand.

The stranger smiled and pointed a gun at them. "Yes, I watched you and the old man hiding the chest several days ago."

"You better hand over the money before I turn you in!"

The thief grabbed the chest, threw a chair at Fuchsia, and cackled as she mounted the window ledge.

Suzanna sprang for her like a cat, causing the two of them to fall to the floor. They knocked over a candle, which set fire to the bed, and Suzanna pushed the gun across the floor with her elbow.

Fuchsia screamed at Suzanna to stop before they burned to death.

Suzanna jumped for the chest and shoved all the money into it.

The thief scratched Suzanna's face and pulled her hair.

Fuchsia helped Suzanna escape from the dreadful mauling. Her face was bloody, and her dress was torn. They coughed and hurried out of the building before the fire consumed them.

Part of the building collapsed as the thief staggered out the door and passed out.

The Long-Kept Secret

By the time Fuchsia and Suzanna returned to the peacefulness of the plantation, the laborers had built shelters for themselves behind the barn. They were the only structures on the plantation. A well-known builder from Charleston placed sketches of the estate in Fuchsia's hands upon their return.

Lord Montgomery had always kept British currency for good luck. During his last trip to America, he took most of his inheritance after his mother died from tuberculosis. She had been bedridden for years before she perished, joining her deceased spouse. She had been a skeptic most of her life, and even though she had never acknowledged God, she kept her beliefs and religious convictions hidden until moments before death came knocking at her door. Fuchsia wondered what her grandparents had been like as she thought of her father's bittersweet memories of his sentimental voyages.

Her ancestors were as distant to her as her future. There were more relevant worries to overcome than worrying about her heritage. However, this heritage filled her with pride and self-confidence.

There was a new life to rebuild. It would take a lot of hard work and perseverance to make everything the way she had dreamed it would be. Her dreams seemed like endless hopes and promises she had made to herself as she sat alone on the hilltop and looked at the desolate plantation.

That night, as Fuchsia slept, she dreamed about the thief standing by her parents' graves. Clothed in sinister black apparel, the woman cackled as she pointed at the graves. Fuchsia woke up in a sweat, gasping for air. She had the same bizarre dreams for many nights. She asked God to clear her thoughts and renew her physical and spiritual strength—and He did.

Contrary to her dreams, there was hope indeed. The nation was ready to be rebuilt far better than before. The worst was over. A new beginning greeted the people. Thousands of Southerners would not open their eyes and hearts to the significant advantages of the Southern and Northern states combining. Furthermore, Fuchsia knew the nation would eventually heal into a more prosperous land. The

Alexandra Lamour

unexpected news of Abraham Lincoln's assassination at Ford Theatre left the nation bewildered.

The cutting of boards, the pounding of nails, and the shouts of laborers echoed throughout the plantation. It was not a quick job. To be finished well, they would have to work with great diligence. Fuchsia and Suzanna inspected every wooden joint sample on the cutting table and chose the best quality for everything contributing to the home's completion.

Fuchsia noticed Suzanna's keen eye for finding fault in almost anything that came across their viewing. "I appreciate your eagerness to assist in the short time that you have been here. I can't tell you how nice it is to have you with us. You are the second pair of eyes I need, especially now."

Suzanna smiled and said, "Thank you, ma'am, for giving me the opportunity to work on the plantation."

"Honey, call me Fuchsia. You could be my younger sister. Our ages are only a few years apart."

The next day, Fuchsia examined catalogs of furniture, oriental rugs, ornaments embellished with precious stones from Europe and Africa, and fabrics of silk, lace, and velvet from Paris. She wanted to make her home the most beautiful and admired in the South, and she was pleased that her money would make it happen. A New York catalog displayed rare pieces of art that were going to be on exhibition for auction at the Corcoran Gallery of Art in Washington the following month.

Maybe I can get away if Suzanna will keep a close eye on things, she thought as she stared at the pictures of Chinese, French, and Italian art. She had always believed art was one of the best ways to preserve the past. Fuchsia had grown to appreciate her parents' taste for fine art.

Despite Fuchsia's wealth, losing her family left a scar on her heart. She hoped she could eventually veil the pain by controlling her emotions. In her mind, blackness had settled over her memories of the old manor. A sense of defeat surrounded her when she recalled her parents, Georgette, and her joyful youth. She tried to shake off the painful memories.

PART II

Chapter 4

1868

Three years had passed since the restoration of the estate began. Mr. Jones had been ill for the past month and slept in the east-end corridor of the estate. The last doctor who gave him a thorough examination had informed Fuchsia that he could do nothing else to prolong his life. Therefore, it was best to keep him as comfortable as possible before passing away.

The late afternoon had dispersed, and dusk would arrive soon. The flood of summer light had begun to disappear. Mr. Jones awkwardly held his cup close to his chin and turned to Fuchsia. He was a source of protection for the women, and he had done more for them than anyone else in his life.

He was too feeble to converse for long periods and used hand and eye movements whenever he grew faint. In addition, a crippling paralysis on the left side of his body had impaired his speech. He seldom spoke clearly, forcing Fuchsia to lean close over him. Over the bed, one of Fuchsia's favorite paintings, *The Sistine Madonna,* Mary held Christ in her eyes as she gazed up to heaven.

After Mr. Jones closed his eyes, Fuchsia went over to the window. "I'll be back later," she stated. She kissed his forehead. A dismal feeling engulfed her as she descended the staircase. The presence of death gave her a void.

In order to find some comfort, she went outside and admired the gorgeous flowers. She chose red roses, purple lilacs, pure white lilies, and sweet-smelling gardenias and placed them in a bunch.

Suzanna hurried into the kitchen and brought back tea to the parlor. She and Fuchsia would socialize there in the afternoons. Her face was as pale as a sheet as she paced the floor, continually peeking out of the window from behind the lace curtain. She looked at the French-styled loveseat and whispered, "Everything in this home matches flawlessly, and it is enough to drive me crazy! Nothing is ever out of place—not even a chair! It reminds me of a museum!"

Fuchsia entered the room with flowers sticking out of the side of her head and put the rest of them in a crystal vase on the piano. "Oh, the tea is ready? Aren't these flowers beautiful?"

Suzanna was irritated, but she smiled as she sipped her tea. She wished she could leave, but then she would have nothing again. At least if she stayed, there would be some hope for her. It would be difficult to survive alone financially, and it would be impossible to have the comforting lifestyle she had grown to love on the plantation.

"Fuchsia?" She took another sip of her tea. "I am very much distressed about the way I've been living." Her face turned red, and she fell to the floor with a thump.

One of the servants, Gertrude, appeared and sent for a doctor.

Suzanna's soft, golden hair and rosy, warm cheeks made her look like an angel.

Fuchsia sobbed unceasingly.

Suzanna partially opened her lips and mumbled incoherently. Her eyes reopened and then rolled in a circular movement before closing again.

Fuchsia slapped Suzanna's face several times and held her hand for close to an hour before the doctor entered the parlor, undertaking whatever urgent measures were required.

When Suzanna awoke in her bed, Fuchsia was standing by the window.

Fuchsia raced to Suzanna's bedside and wiped her bloodshot eyes with a damp handkerchief. She took her soft white hand, held it tightly, and prayed for God to care for her.

While Fuchsia explained all the details, Suzanna's eyes widened, and she began to sweat and shake convulsively.

The nurse explained how the water in the well had been tainted. Since the servants usually prepared the meals, Suzanna was unaware that the water was contaminated. She turned her head away, feeling too weak to even be in Fuchsia's loving presence. This woman loved her so much, felt great sympathy, and had watched over her like God's apostle. Fuchsia was ministering to Suzanna's soul.

Fright filled Suzanna's mind as she thought of dying. Something told her she would die, and no one could save her—not even Dr. Bridge. She screamed for help, but it was useless. There was no comfort anywhere.

Fuchsia and the nurse continued their conversation.

"Try to drink this." The nurse held a glass against Suzanna's trembling lips. "The doctor believes you will recover soon."

Suzanna struggled to speak because the pain in her throat was excruciating.

Fuchsia reappeared at her bedside, stroked her curls, and smiled.

After a week, Fuchsia mentioned that she needed a break from life on the plantation.

Alexandra Lamour

Suzanna thought, *She has to be out of her mind. I would never take a trip with her. Her innocence blinds her!*

Mr. Jones' bedroom was empty as Suzanna passed it on her way to the staircase. It had been several days since the funeral. She had been the first to discover that he had died. The horrible expression on his face would linger in her mind forever. His face had been yellowish, and his bulging eyes were fixed on the upper-right side of the room. He had suffered for four months, but he had never complained or criticized the doctors and nurses for laboring in vain to restore him to the man he had once been. Instead, he accepted death with serenity. He had always ensured that Suzanna and Fuchsia were looked after. The women had looked up to him with great respect.

Suzanna's health had been almost completely restored. She gazed at her face in the hallway mirror. Her decreased weight brought her much apprehension. She remembered the terror she had experienced in the orphanage when she had gone without food for a few days. Suzanna would not let herself become a bag of bones again.

She walked down the vast staircase, ignoring the priceless art on the chestnut walls. The clicking sound of her heels echoed on each step as she descended. The sound of her heels intensified as she approached the foyer.

A maid was dusting off a brass clock on the small table by the parlor door, ignoring the approaching sound of her heels.

"Where's Fuchsia?" Suzanna asked.

The maid turned around with a startled glance toward the parlor. The staff did not care for Suzanna's stoic personality. She was so unlike Fuchsia.

Suzanna was standing by the maid in her emerald green dress and high heels as Fuchsia entered the parlor. Her tangled hair had been combed and hung loosely on her full breasts. Her lips were painted bright red. Suzanna turned to Fuchsia, and their eyes met. Her eyes were cold and angry.

Suzanna said, "I'm going away, Fuchsia. I need a vacation. I have decided to go to Europe."

The Long-Kept Secret

"Oh, come in, my dear. Sit down. It is so nice to see that you are feeling better. I'm so glad your speech has come back."

"Fuchsia, I am much better. I am planning on leaving on Friday. A train leaves for New York every Friday at seven o'clock in the morning."

"Suzanna, you need to rest more. You are still not well. I can't let you leave so soon, especially not on your own. I forbid it!"

"You forbid it? How can you forbid it? I have the right to come and go as I please!" Suzanna knew she had the upper hand since Fuchsia had told her on many occasions she helped replace a dark void in her life. Suzanna turned and left the room.

Friday morning came quicker than Fuchsia had anticipated. When she returned from her daily visit to Mr. Jones' tombstone, her body became lethargic. As she drew nearer to the carriage, she felt depressed. She had been wearing the same black dress for two weeks. When the carriage departed for the train station loneliness overcame her. It was a feeling that she had not experienced in a long time.

A messenger on a horse passed the spectacular carriage on his way to Montgomery's plantation.

Fuchsia stood on the veranda with the letter in her shaking hand, shocked and overjoyed by such marvelous news. It was true! Suzanna was her half-sister! The tombstone that was, by chance, dug up by the gardener during the burial of Mr. Jones had brought some suspicions to light. She recalled the night when Georgette had faithfully brought the mysterious flowers to her sister Priscilla's grave, Suzanna's mother, on her birthday. The orphanage gave all the pertinent information needed to confirm Priscilla was indeed her mother.

The detailed letter from Mrs. Silver, an employee at the orphanage, said that Suzanna's mother was Montgomery's most favored African American servant. Mrs. Silver worked at the orphanage for more

Alexandra Lamour

than thirty years. She was present when Priscilla arrived. During the evening, she helped deliver Suzanna.

Priscilla told Mrs. Silver about her affair with Lord Montgomery. She had departed from her duties when she discovered she was with child. Their romantic relationship was hidden for more than a year. After Suzanna's birth, her mother's poor health and excessive bleeding led to her death the following day. The baby remained in the orphanage without Lord Montgomery's knowledge. Georgette and Lady Montgomery had kept their secret until their deaths. It was an enlightening letter.

Fuchsia was ecstatic about the news and paid little attention to Suzanna's illegitimate birth. She had family, and Suzanna was her sister, which counted most. She had to get to the station before the train left! She had to stop the train!

Chapter 5

Suzanna boarded the train, relieved that she was going far away from Charleston. She wished for a new start. She needed a break from it all. Luckily, she had saved up enough money over the years from Fuchsia for household and gardening services. Her appetite grew while sitting in the dining room and examining a menu written in French and English.

The waiter stood over her as she ordered her meal.

"I would like *la soupe aux legumes avec sauce béchamel*. It sounds delicious. And *monsieur, tarte aux pommes* for dessert, *merci*."

"Oui, mademoiselle, merci." He clicked his heels together, bowed his head, and left.

Suzanna drank some tea to alleviate the pain in her throat. She was glad that most of the redness on her neck from the tainted well water had disappeared. She pulled up her collar to hide a little scarring and searched for the mirror in her purse to arrange her hat. After fiddling with it for some time, she tossed it off her head, permitting her hair to fall loosely upon her shoulders. She went over her itinerary before her lunch arrived, making last-minute changes for her convenience. *I'll be gone for several weeks*, she pondered. *It'll give me plenty of time to reexamine my life. My life needs to change.* Unless she became a shrewd businesswoman, she would always remain submissive to somebody else. The thought of living such a

Alexandra Lamour

life infuriated her. She smacked her lips and ate the scrumptious food placed before her.

When Suzanna finally arrived in New York, she went to the Fifth Avenue Hotel, situated in the heart of the city. It had an entire block of frontage and was between Twenty-Third Street and Twenty-Fourth Street. She would take a ship to Marseilles, France. France was an enchanted country that she had only read about in books, and she longed to visit.

She gracefully got out of the carriage, walked to the main lobby door, and dropped her glove on the way to the front desk. She was unaware that the accidental drop of her glove would change her destiny. When she turned around to retrieve it, she was spellbound.

A handsome, tall, slender man held her silk glove. He was good-looking with dark, inviting eyes. His fair hair was well-groomed. His face beamed with success and self-confidence.

"Thank you," she responded.

"Edward O'Reilly," he said as he removed his hat and shook her hand.

"Suzanna Smith." She turned around, hoping he would speak to her again.

"I hope I'm not being presumptuous, but I would like to invite you to dinner. There's a quaint restaurant within walking distance."

"Mr. O'Reilly, thank you, but I don't know you."

He chuckled. "Well, what better way to get to know each other."

She coolly accepted, moved by his sophisticated appearance. It was hard to believe she had fallen for a stranger in such a short time, which sparked a desire for a passionate love affair.

At half past six, a gentle knock on Suzanna's door caused her heart to flutter as she glimpsed at her fancy dress in the mirror. She found her matching handbag on the dresser and said, "One moment, please."

The Long-Kept Secret

She opened the door and walked to his side, spellbound by his good looks. His formal attire was impressive.

"My, you look lovely," he stated. "Shall we."

"Yes. of course."

When they arrived at the restaurant, the maitre d' quickly led them to a table in the corner.

Suzanna smiled, which caused her eyes to sparkle, paralleling the glittering jewels on her ears and neck that Fuchsia had given her over the years. While at the table, the customers gazed at her.

"You are beautiful and witty," Edward said. "You are getting a lot of attention. You are what I have been searching for all my life."

"Amazing how you can know so much about someone in such a short time," she said, enjoying his flattery.

"I believe that our eyes are the mirrors of our souls and can tell us astounding wonders about ourselves." He continued to charm Suzanna. "I know more about you than you know about yourself."

"Oh, do you?" She giggled as she looked at her envious onlookers. "I think I already know your profession. You are a fortune teller."

"Wrong." He chuckled. "I'm a landowner. I buy up land in the South and then sell it to the Northerners to make a handsome profit. I am here for another week to close a deal with the Harrisburg Contracting Company, and then I'll be on my way back home."

Suzanna felt far away from him for a while, and she regretted inquiring about his personal life. She tried to modify the conversation.

"I'm looking forward to visiting France."

Edward responded, "I have yet to go to Europe myself. I've been too busy here to have taken the initiative to go overseas. I've got to get back to Charleston as soon as possible to close another deal. I haven't been there in over a year."

"Charleston?" she said, trying to cover her surprise.

"Yes. Have you been there before, Suzanna?"

"Once … in my childhood, but that was a long time ago." She sipped some red wine. Since she was unsure of his intent, she refrained from giving him too much personal information.

Alexandra Lamour

After dinner, they took a stroll in Manhattan. The air was fresh and crisp. It smelled like spring and felt like summer was approaching soon. The full moon radiated in the dark sky.

What an excellent time to fall in love, Suzanna thought as they turned around and headed back toward the hotel. "My, it is a beautiful evening. Are there any interesting places to visit in New York? I've heard the newly constructed Metropolitan Museum of Art is a sight to see."

"Yes, but I'm not really into art." He chuckled and rubbed his mustache. "Chilly?" He placed his arm around Suzanna's delicate shoulder.

"Oh, a little." She glanced up at his face, desiring a kiss.

His perfectly straight nose looked like an artist had carved it. His skin was without blemish. When he smiled, his lips were firmly closed, rarely showing his teeth.

Suzanna thought of postponing her trip for another week. To miss an opportunity to spend time in the company of such a man would be a mistake.

"I'll be leaving next week," Edward said. "When are you departing for France?"

"Next Friday. Ships are now departing once a week."

She knew it would be to her advantage to defer her trip to get to know him better. Her chances of meeting a man of such intelligence, wealth, and good looks were rare. Suzanna could not find anything about him that she did not like.

Edward displayed no change in emotion as she spoke about her itinerary overseas. She suddenly felt nervous and uncomfortable. The streetlights lit up their faces as they passed the park. She was unfulfilled. She had wanted him to fall in love with her. She thought about her unreserved questioning and impulsive acceptance of dinner and was angry with herself. She wanted to tear off her dress when she returned to her room. She hated the way her hair was styled. Also, her cosmetics were too heavily applied. *I have made a spectacle of myself!* she thought.

As they ascended the stairs into the lobby, he asked, "Would you like to have dinner tomorrow? I know a great outdoor restaurant close by?"

"Oh, that would be lovely."

He walked her to her room and kissed her lips gently. It was her first kiss. Her body experienced novel sensations that awakened her female desires.

The next evening, they walked back to the hotel after dinner.

"How about a nightcap? It always warms the body and promotes better sleep, especially on a chilly night."

Without hesitating, she said, "I would like that."

This time, he looked into her yearning eyes, which she tried to cover up with a quick smile. She hastily accepted since she did not have a desire to refuse him.

It was inappropriate for a lady to go to a man's room unescorted, and she began to scold herself for accepting. *I'm sure he can see right through me,* she believed. His age and life experiences enthralled her. She was new at the game of love and would be clay in his hands. She felt helplessly overtaken by desire.

When he opened the door to his room, he would have an advantage over her since she longed for an accomplished man to be in control of her feelings. Suzanna knew Edward would win in the end, and she refrained from refusing him. She had never allowed herself to fall for a man. *There is no stopping now,* she reassured herself, since she needed him more than he needed her.

He prevailed over her as he locked the door, and his masculinity awakened her. Edward's gestures and words told her he was a man who had romanced many women in his lifetime, which she found so alluring. His calm demeanor was exciting.

Suzanna feared revealing her vulnerability to him since she always had control of her emotions. She knew he had her under his

Alexandra Lamour

magical powers as he reached leisurely for the wine bottle and crystal glasses on the table. "I have white or red wine. However, I think Zinfandel from Napa Valley surpasses any international red wine."

"Well, you've convinced me. I'll take a glass of Zinfandel." She reached for her glass. "I think you are a wine expert."

"Not really, but I do enjoy quality wines." He sat beside her and caressed the back of her head.

The wine and the fire filled her with anticipation.

Edward filled their glasses a second time. He whispered soothing words about how her beauty overtook him as he kissed her dainty neck, causing a tingling sensation throughout her body.

Suzanna wanted to faint as she became weaker. Female feelings ran rampant throughout her body.

His fingers ran down her spine.

She relaxed, yearning for him to continue, but something told her she would be making a mistake if she submitted to him. She turned her head away.

"What is it?" he asked.

"I don't know you well enough, Edward. You don't know me. I haven't even told you about myself. I shouldn't have accepted your invitation. You must be thinking I'm a harlot." She blushed and stood on unsteady feet.

She wanted him even more. She walked over to the table and filled her glass. "I think I have had too much wine."

"OK." He took the glass from her hand. "Yes, that's plenty for now. Come and sit down. I wouldn't want you to fall."

"I'm fine. Honestly." She belched loudly, causing them to laugh.

Alcohol was confusing her mind. He had seen another side of her. He had known her true colors all along. She was no different from the women in his past.

Edward gently held her arms, told her to relax, and kissed her forehead. He then put his lips on hers with such warmth and force that she relinquished herself to him. He carried her helpless, limp body to the inviting bed, touched her hair lightly, and slowly kissed her shoulders.

30

The Long-Kept Secret

When he undid the buttons on the back of her dress, she lost control. She caressed and kissed his firm shoulders as she unfastened the buttons of his shirt.

Struggling to release the shirt's cuff, he grinned. "It won't come off."

"Let me help you." She laughed again, pulling it off and feeling slightly intoxicated. She knew his manly instinct was alive, and she would try to be fascinating in every way.

He knew she was new at the game of love. He was gentle and provocative, and he took his time to teach her the pleasures of the body.

"Kiss me again." His warm lips aroused her remarkably.

"You are striking and irresistible." He fulfilled her request.

There was no turning back now; she had succumbed to his will. His physique and fragrance stimulated her womanly passions even more. If she could have melted in his arms, she would have. He began kissing her face and then every inch of her arm as he descended her body. He noticed she was in ecstasy and would satisfy him fully.

Edward was a man of adventure, which triggered every nerve in her being. He knew what she wanted to feel, and he knew what she wanted to hear. He had a talent and magnetism for charming any woman.

"Edward, you are remarkable. Don't stop now."

"And you are delightful, my dear. Let me have my way with you so I can please you. Let me kiss you all over your body."

Suzanna believed she was falling madly in love. He was everything she had ever wanted in life. She didn't know what tomorrow would bring, but she couldn't think of a better place than in Edward's comforting arms. The euphoria of lovemaking intensified throughout the night.

He blew out the candle by the bed.

Chapter 6

The following morning, when Suzanna awoke, Edward was reading the *New York Times* at the table by the open window while smoking a cigar. Coffee and toast with orange marmalade were on a silver tray. Suzanna got out of bed and helped herself to coffee. "Good morning. I can't start my day without coffee."

"Good morning, my dear. I thought you were going to sleep all day." He smirked.

"I was tempted. I haven't slept like that in ages." She put on her robe and headed for the lavatory. "I am going to wash up and perhaps take a bath."

He approached her and placed her in his arms. "Don't be too long." He kissed the top of her head. "You are ravishing."

"Oh, Edward, such flattery will get you so far. I'll be back soon, and I hope you can plan today's attractions. I know there are some fun places to visit in New York … before I head overseas … and you head down to Charleston."

"What do you think of Central Park? I've heard it's great this time of year."

"Sounds good to me." She took a large towel, her favorite perfume oil, and a change of clothing. She was relieved the lavatory was empty. She filled the bathtub with a bucket of hot water and reached for a bar of tallow soap to wash her body and hair. Then she immersed her body into the tub and dreamed of her life with Edward.

32

The Long-Kept Secret

He was more than she could have ever imagined. The water soothed her body and mind, making her feel relaxed. She was such a lucky woman now that she had met him. Her heart did not regret giving herself to him because she had fallen head over heels in love. He was a magnificent lover. Instead, she envisioned their marriage. The church was ornate with colorful stained glass windows and flowers along the aisles. She saw herself in a glorious white wedding dress and Edward standing beside her in a three-piece suit and a Chesterfield coat. *Fuchsia will be my maid of honor. I'm sure she would approve of him,* she thought. They would probably live in a beautiful home in New York and have two or three children. He would be a nurturing father. She snapped her mind back to reality and decided to get out of the tub.

The long bath was a great idea because it comforted her body and mind. She anointed herself with perfume oil, covering her body from head to toe. She brushed her hair and tried to dry it near the stove, and then she squeezed the ends with the towel to allow her natural curls to form. After some time, she applied cosmetics to give her face some color. Finally, she put on her clothes, realizing she had taken longer than planned.

When she returned to the room, Edward was dressed and drinking coffee by the window. "For heaven's sake, I thought you had drowned in there. I was just about to check on you."

"Well, how do I look?" She turned around so he could get a good look at her in her sky blue dress.

"Splendid, I must say. You are a sight for sore eyes. And as for the perfume, I can smell it over here." He chuckled.

"I hope you like it."

"Now, what wouldn't I like about you?" He beamed. "We better get out of here before I lose my senses again." His embrace gave her a feeling of protection.

"Edward, I love your sense of humor." She took his hand as they left for the park.

Central Park had been completed in 1858, making it a novel and relaxing place to visit, especially for visitors. Suzanna loved to pack

Alexandra Lamour

lunches, a trait that she had acquired from the plantation's cook. Edward purchased a picnic basket, and Suzanna packed a perfect lunch with different kinds of cheeses, meats, whole wheat bread, three bottles of soda water, and freshly baked peach cobbler from the General Store of Manhattan, which was close to their hotel.

"I must say, we have a feast." He reached for the glasses. "Better than drinking from a bottle."

"I've done this so many times that I could do it with my eyes closed."

Suzanna wore her laced-up heeled boots because Edward was so tall. Her parasol matched her flashy flowered dress and bonnet. She linked her arm to his as they walked down Forty-Second Street, just west of Park Avenue. Proud to have Edward by her side, she noticed a few women admiring him as they passed by. One of them glared at Suzanna's revealing dress. Their enviousness gave her a feeling of triumph since she enjoyed flaunting her seductive body and beauty. At the same time, Edward's good looks and confident appearance always drew the attention of females. The walk would take twenty minutes, and she soon regretted wearing her boots.

"I hope the new asphalt sidewalks aren't too uncomfortable for your feet," he said. "Sure beats wooden sidewalks. Do you want me to carry you, my sweetheart? I think you are having a time in those high-heeled boots."

"It's not necessary, I'm fine." She lied since she didn't want to be a nuisance. It was the first time he had called her sweetheart, which was music to her ears.

When they reached their destination, a talented artist sketched them for a reasonable price. He had them sit on a bench overlooking a peaceful lake. Edward handed the drawing to Suzanna; it was a keepsake for her to remember an unforgettable day.

"Now, does that look like me?" She frowned. "It definitely looks like you."

"My face looks bigger than it is," he stated.

Edward found a partially shady spot near the lake to sit. She laid a white tablecloth on the grass and put down the picnic basket under

The Long-Kept Secret

her parasol. Then she filled two glasses of soda water to the top to quench their thirst. He picked white daffodils from a bush and placed one in her hair. Suzanna thanked him by wrapping her arms around his neck, causing him to fall forward.

"Sorry, I didn't mean that." She laughed.

"I guess I'm falling for you. Well, I must say, you are spoiling me."

"And why shouldn't I?"

She put a piece of cheese in his mouth.

"Well, I love every minute of it. Please continue."

She rubbed his back and told him to lie down in her lap. "You work too hard. You need to relax more often."

"I must say, I definitely agree with you."

He closed his eyes as she massaged the sides of his face. She teased him about a few gray hairs at the back of his head. Then she toyed with the ends of his curled-up mustache.

"They are signs of wisdom, my dear. And hard work. Don't mock me."

Suzanna's sweet voice hummed a melody.

"You have a nice voice."

"Do you really like it?" she inquired.

"Absolutely."

"Hungry?"

"I didn't eat breakfast."

She made sandwiches, meticulously folding the cheeses and meats between two thick pieces of bread, and handed him one. Immediately, he placed part of his sandwich in her mouth, and she did the same for him. They both laughed childishly.

Birds flocked above them as Suzanna threw crumbs in the air. They chirped over their heads as though celebrating the couple's enjoyable time together. She wanted to ask him about his true feelings toward her—her heart yearned for his love—but she wondered if she was being hasty.

"Edward," she began and she straightened her posture. "I hope we will see each other again when I return from France. I'm enjoying our time together."

Alexandra Lamour

He pulled her close, kissed her passionately, and said, "Let fate make that decision." He looked stern and detached. His silence concerned her.

Suzanna sensed Edward was a man who found it difficult to stay in relationships for a long time because he was always traveling for his business. He informed her about his previous affairs, which were all short-term ones. She hoped their relationship would be different and would last forever.

"This is what I love about traveling. There are so many interesting places and people to meet. Like you," he stated as they boarded a carriage for the hotel.

"Who was your last lover?" she inquired with reluctance.

"Now, let me think this over." He smiled. "It began yesterday."

She had a solemn expression. "Are you being honest with me? Are you sure?" Her amorous eyes revealed her weakness for him. She assumed he couldn't make commitments that confined him, which would eventually lead to setbacks. Edward was very special to her, and she believed it was best not to create false expectations. To avoid having her heart broken, she refrained from sharing what she truly felt.

Suzanna attempted to fill in the gaps in their relationship by putting the scattered pieces together. He was a puzzle to her. *Where is it going from here?* she wondered. She felt an urge to flee quickly, but something held her back. His presence filled a relentless vacuum of unresolved wounds and loneliness from her childhood. *Maybe he is the key to my true happiness.*

In the evening, they attended a show at the Bowery Theatre, which had opened in 1826. It was located in the Bowery on the Lower East Side of Manhattan and was filled with people of all ages.

"I saw the daring trapeze artists, Francois and August Siegrist, perform several months ago. They have packed the theater every night. Their original harrowing acts always leave the audiences breathless."

"Oh my!" she shouted. "I can't look at the man walking on a tightrope thirty feet from the ground!"

The Long-Kept Secret

Edward laughed, covering her eyes with his hands. "Don't worry, they are well-trained performers, and they won't get hurt."

They watched close to an hour of riveting performances, enjoying the next one more than the prior one. The final act caused everyone to gasp with fear, making the show spectacular.

In the late evening, Suzanna dressed in a lace nightgown that Edward bought her. He smoked a cigar in his pajama trousers by the lit fireplace. His presence fascinated her. He rose to meet her halfway across the room and kissed her with all the fervor of a man. Then he picked her up in his strong arms and carried her to the bed. They indulged in romantic lovemaking as the flickering flames danced to the rhythm of the night. Suzanna knew she would be shattered if their relationship terminated. It was the first time in her life that she felt alive. When Edward fell asleep, she whispered loving words in his ear. She lay by him, enjoying the sound of his breathing and his body's warmth, and placed her arms around him. *I could lay like this forever,* she pondered. She wished for a marriage proposal.

The next day, they decided to visit Manhattan Beach, a little over an hour's drive from the city. They left in the early morning to avoid the heat and crowds. Upon arrival, Suzanna picked up a pamphlet at a stand along the beach walkway.

She read, "Austin Corbin, the founder of the beach, recently began investing in the area when a doctor told him the ocean would improve his son's health." She turned to signal it was his turn to read.

Edward leaned over her shoulder and said, "Within a few years, lavish hotels and restaurants will be added, making it a fancy getaway for New Yorkers."

She added, "A place for the rich to relax and forget about the city's stress. Everyone could use a little relaxation."

Suzanna changed into a white bathing corset and carried a matching parasol to protect her delicate skin. Her provocative apparel gathered the attention of many sunbathers and swimmers. Edward wore a pair of long red-and-white-striped drawers. She giggled at the large weights sewn into his swimsuit's hems so they would not rise in the water.

37

Alexandra Lamour

They walked along the shoreline hand in hand, sharing their dreams and laughing at life and its absurdities. The ocean was serene and invigorating.

A large tree shaded them from the sun, and Suzanna laid down a large towel. She napped on Edward's lap, enjoying the rhythmic sound of the ocean. Later on, Edward invited Suzanna to swim by tugging at her arm and teasing her.

"It's much too cold," she said. "Please, no, I can't get in the water."

"I'll warm you up." He approached her in an attempt to carry her into the water.

"No, Edward!" she shouted, drawing the attention of the other swimmers.

"OK." He laughed. "Hungry?"

"Famished."

He led her to a street vendor with a pushcart. They ordered sodas and hot dogs, and then he surprised her with lemon-flavored ice cream.

"My, this is so sweet but tasty. I love the flavor." She handed him the rest of the hot dog. "I am not too keen about the hot dog."

"The vendor told me hot dogs will be a fast-food sensation for Americans one day," he stated.

"That's hard to believe. It has such an unusual taste. I think it takes time to get accustomed to it."

After a few hours at the beach, the sun began to disappear—and they were left alone. The beach was desolate and suddenly became chilly.

He laid her back in his arms and kissed her playfully. She didn't want him to release her. She wanted to tell him she adored him, but she couldn't find the right words.

"It's getting dark. We better head back," he said while pulling on his trousers. "I hope it won't be difficult to find a carriage this late at the beach."

"I'm sure there will be one available." She slid her dress over her bathing corset. "I loved the entire day."

"Every day is a new day with you, Suzanna."

38

The Long-Kept Secret

Her tender eyes watched him advance a carriage. He always knew what to say at the best time.

They boarded a carriage to return to the hotel. Edward had promised a special dinner, and they needed to prepare before dark.

In the evening, Edward surprised Suzanna with a stunning dress purchased from the renowned Lord & Taylor department store on Broadway at Grant Street. Its emerald sequins shimmered, and the pearled neckline was the focal point. It was the most stylish and risqué dress she had ever seen. The semicircular neckline accentuated her bosom.

"Oh, Edward! It fits me perfectly! How did you know my size? It must have cost you a fortune." She turned around to view the exquisite tight-fitting material that revealed her curves. The fancy sterling buttons on the back enhanced its style. She pulled down the sleeves to show off her bare shoulders. Then she looked over at Edward to see his reaction. He bowed his head in approval. "I will always cherish this dress. It's more than I ever anticipated."

"You sure are as pretty as a picture." He walked over to her for a kiss. "My, you truly look radiant tonight."

"You are the most handsome man I've ever met," she responded. His gray suit and top hat gave him the appearance of a gentleman.

He grabbed her arms and pulled her under his chin, holding her tight. "I might never let you go," he whispered.

Suzanna's heart soared with delight, and she kept quiet in case his words were just words and nothing more.

"Shall we go, Miss Smith?"

"Absolutely, Mr. O'Reilly."

It was a splendid night as they traveled by horse and carriage to a cozy restaurant on South William Street, Delmonico, which had opened in 1838. It was usually packed every night and required reservations.

"You will love this restaurant," he began.

She gazed at him as the carriage came to a halt. His white shirt enhanced his stunning tan. He looked about the street and commented,

"It's the birthplace of the Delmonico steak. Abraham Lincoln was a fan of the mashed potatoes topped with cheese and bread crumbs."

"I'm impressed by your knowledge of so many fine places in New York." She smiled, admiring his worldliness.

Edward and Suzanna shared a steak and a large plate of mashed potatoes. She loved the savory red wine that topped off the meal. Most of all, she favored how the customers sat in small groups around the restaurant, and their loud voices offset the acoustics; something she had never seen at home. The nightlife and liveliness of the people made New York the most thrilling city; Charleston seemed so laid back and simple.

When the music commenced, the chattering declined as kerosene lamps lit up the corner of the restaurant. The pianist bowed his head at a lively couple in approval as they spiced up the evening with rhythmic dance moves. Other couples joined in the merriment.

Edward rose and reached out his hand for Suzanna's. "My, you are light on your feet, my darling," he whispered in her ear and then released her as he turned her in small circles.

"You are quite the dancer, Edward."

After dessert, they decided to walk before taking the carriage back to the hotel since it was a starry night. Suzanna wanted to tell Edward how deeply she cared for him. Above all, he was the first man she had grown so close to in such a short time—and had shared intimacy. She looked at his profile as he gazed silently in deep thought. *What is he thinking? Has he enjoyed the evening as much as I have? Is this the beginning or the end of our relationship? Did he recently have a lover?* He looked disturbed, and she wanted him to confide in her.

"A penny for your thoughts."

"Oh, I was just thinking about something. It's not important."

They boarded a carriage and headed for the hotel. She couldn't hold back her feelings any longer and finally said, "I can't help but notice you are in deep thought." She looked into his warm eyes. "Tell me what's on your mind."

"Just thinking about tomorrow's meeting. It is business, and I don't want to trouble you with that now. Let us enjoy what's left of the evening." He pulled her closer and kissed her hand.

"Everything will go well for you tomorrow. By the way, thank you for such a wonderful time. The dinner was delicious."

"Yes, I always go to Delmonico on my business trips. I haven't had a dissatisfied dinner yet." He caressed her shoulder and then placed her shawl over it.

The next morning, when Suzanna awoke, Edward had already left for his meeting. She quickly washed up in the basin and put on the prettiest pink dress in her wardrobe. Then she slipped on matching high-heeled shoes with large bows over the ankles. She brushed her hair meticulously and then applied her cosmetics lightly since she knew Edward preferred a more natural appearance during the day.

To her amazement, Edward was already in the hallway. She heard him telling the maid to bring more towels to his room.

When the door opened, Suzanna leaped for him at the doorway, surprising him.

"Well, good morning, my dear. You startled me. I didn't expect you to be lurking at the doorway."

"That was the idea." She laughed.

"Another beautiful dress. It will surely be a head-turner."

She looked at him coyly. "Your compliments are spoiling me."

"Well, the deal went well." He picked her up, and they turned around joyfully. "It was luck, sheer luck. I almost lost the deal to a Southerner who owned less land."

"I told you it would work out."

"A very wealthy New Yorker wants fifty acres just outside of Charleston for mining phosphate and manufacturing factories. Phosphate is used frequently now for fertilizers." He paused and sat down on the sofa. "I'm glad to get that off my chest."

Alexandra Lamour

"I'm sure you made a bundle of money," she said, pleased to see he was in a good mood.

"He gave me 50 percent, and I will receive the other half in Charleston. I must say, this is my most profitable deal. It looks like you bring me good luck, young lady."

"I'm happy to hear that." She watched as he stood up and tossed the money on the bed. "I've never seen that much money at one time." Her face beamed with delight.

He picked up the bundle of bills in rubber bands and placed them in a small metal vault secured by a combination lock.

"Breakfast awaits you in the dining room. Shall we?"

"Yes, I'm ravenous."

"Tonight we will celebrate at a popular restaurant in the city. It's near New York Harbor.

"Which one?"

"It's a surprise. I hope you like seafood."

"All kinds." Her eyes lit up with enthusiasm.

He pulled out his Swiss pocket watch from his late father and gazed at the time.

After breakfast, they returned to the room and made love. His desire for her was more intense than the former evenings, and she enjoyed every minute of it. As they lay quietly in each other's arms, Suzanna again wanted to express her love for him. Instead, she continued to keep her sentiments bottled up.

"Let's stay in bed all day."

"Wishful thinking," he said with a grin. "There is always something to do. I will be back shortly. Be sure to be all dolled up by the time I return." He kissed her.

"Another meeting?"

He frowned.

"Everything will go well for you. You are probably a great negotiator."

"Now, how do you know that?"

He touched her dainty nose and kissed it.

"You are a man of many talents," she replied.

42

It was apparent how much Edward was growing fond of Suzanna. She believed he didn't tell her he was falling in love with her due to his pride. *Perhaps the timing was wrong*, she thought. Then her perception of him quickly shifted as she viewed him from the window walking alone. A surge of jealousy filled her heart. *I hope he is not meeting another woman. Heavens no! Then I would be a fool!* She hastily dismissed the idea from her mind before it enraged her.

After dinner, they headed back to the hotel. Suzanna was in deep contemplation and wanted to know Edward's true intentions. It was tearing her apart inside. Unable to withhold her feelings anymore, she asked, "When will we see each other again?" She turned her head in his direction, hoping for a positive response.

"Tomorrow sounds good to me. I have a short business meeting, but we can meet in the afternoon if you wish."

They embraced as the carriage passed Central Park, which was beautiful at night. Suzanna felt the abundant gas streetlights were impressive since they brought such illumination to the city. A dark shadow covered them along Fifth Avenue, not far from the hotel, and they shared a long kiss, which left her breathless. Her urges for him grew, and she yearned to be his wife even more. She wanted him to be committed to her.

Fear overcame her when she thought of their upcoming separation, and she dreaded it terribly. Trying not to get caught up in her emotions, she took a deep breath to calm her thoughts. Finally, Suzanna couldn't hold back her feelings and said, "You didn't understand my question. I hope we can see each other again when I return from Europe." She did not understand Edward at all. He had repeatedly told her how lovely she was, but to her misfortune, she knew he was only available for a short time. She could tell by his tone of voice that she was probably nothing more to him than a short engagement. He did not know what she felt. He was too reserved and

Alexandra Lamour

in charge of his feelings. Suzanna wasn't his first relationship, and she wouldn't be his last. He hadn't committed to her happiness, and he continued to look away.

Her eyes filled with sorrow, and she blurted out boldly, "You never planned on seeing me once I returned from overseas, did you? Please tell me, Edward!"

He took in a deep breath and slowly exhaled. She believed he didn't want to totally destroy the evening. He looked at her calmly, maintaining his composure. Avoiding answering her question spoke to her, clearly showing the truth of his intent.

"I'm in love with you, Edward!" she exclaimed, trying to calm down. "I can't figure out any of this, but the one thing I do know is that I want to be with you. I hope you will say I love you too." She wiped the tears from her cheeks and saw that her cosmetics had stained her gloves. Yet she didn't care about her appearance. Ultimately, she had fully exposed herself to him, and he knew what was truly in her heart. She was an open book since he could read her thoughts. He held the dice in his hands. Edward granted passionate lovemaking to women to satisfy his needs only. Commitments were unthinkable.

Suzanna reached for the driver's hand as she exited the carriage. She was embarrassed that the driver had overheard their conversation and would probably later mock her behavior. She didn't notice Edward paying him as she rushed dishearteningly into the hotel. She avoided making a spectacle of herself in the lobby. Then she headed for the elevator, and the door closed quickly.

She hurried to her room, kicked off her shoes, and fell on the bed in despair. To avoid damaging her dress, she undressed and slipped on her robe. Rejection was so painful. Her insecurities from the past had a hold of her now. She had never felt her parents' love, and memories of the orphanage's neglect had traumatized her, which usually resurfaced negative feelings when she faced rejection. A deep sense of abandonment had haunted her for years. Suzanna craved love with a man so dearly. Edward represented a purpose in her life, a direction, and stability! He was her hope. He was her everything.

The Long-Kept Secret

The flickering lights from the adjacent hotel lit up her room, mimicking her stirred-up emotions. She sat near the window, took a deep breath, and regained some self-control. When she heard knocking, she walked to the door. Then she leaned her back against it.

Edward called to her in a regretful tone. "Suzanna, open the door."

"Go away. Leave me alone."

"You are overreacting. Please open the door." She could hear his heavy breathing and the frustration in his voice. "I need to talk to you."

"Are you involved with another woman?"

"No. Why would you believe that nonsense?"

"You are holding back your true emotions."

There was silence for a minute.

"There's no point continuing, Edward."

"I don't want it to end like this, Suzanna."

She did not respond.

The knocking continued a little longer and then stopped, and she felt her heart skip a beat. It was over. There was no reason to talk to him. Deep down in her heart, she knew she was right. They were like two ships passing in the night. The room felt empty, causing her heart to ache terribly. The light across the street flickered on her face as she rose from the bed. She approached the window and spotted Edward walking down the street. His clasped hands rested on the lower part of his back. She wondered where he was going alone and in the middle of the night. He stopped under the kerosene lamp to look at his pocket watch and then disappeared around the corner. There was a sudden urge to pursue him. While in deep contemplation, she decided to remain in her room.

When morning arrived, Suzanna could not rid herself of her feelings for Edward. Exhausted from lack of sleep, she hastily dressed and went to his room, but there was no answer. When she hurried down to the dining room, hoping to see him, he was not there. Her eyes glanced about the lobby, and she recalled his comment about leaving in about a week.

Alexandra Lamour

Suzanna approached the desk clerk.

"Miss, can I help you?"

"Yes, I'm looking for Mr. O'Reilly. By chance, have you seen him this morning?"

The clerk surveyed a registration book. "One moment please, ma'am." His finger stopped midway on the page. "Yes, he mentioned an early meeting before leaving. I must say he appeared quite disturbed about something." The clerk paused. "Oh yes, I recall now, he decided to head to Charleston earlier than planned." He turned the book in her direction and pointed to his exit time.

Regret filled her mind and heart as she thought of her behavior the previous night. She had ruined everything. Whatever hope she had for them of ever being together had been destroyed. She should have opened the door. Hastiness was one of her weaknesses. Suzanna had let her emotions get the best of her, which she had never done before. Edward had awakened her feelings. He had touched the depths of her heart.

She wondered why he had left so rapidly if she was the one for him. He didn't even say goodbye, not giving her a second chance. Now that he was out of reach, getting him back was impossible. She forced herself to admit he wasn't coming back for her. He was gone. Suzanna went back to speak with the concierge. "Sir, by chance, do you have the schedule for ships departing for France?"

"I believe they leave once a week now. Friday is the next one." He handed her a schedule.

"I will be checking out Friday instead of next week," she said.

"OK, Miss Smith. I'll be sure to have the porter collect your baggage, and a carriage will be scheduled for your departure early on Friday morning. Is six o'clock in the morning OK?"

"Yes, that will give me plenty of time to get to New York Harbor."

She returned to her room to pack a few of her belongings that she would no longer have use of. She tossed a couple of souvenirs into her baggage. She felt frustrated and disappointed by how things had ended. Her mind raced with thoughts of bewilderment. For some time, she believed it would be better to go after Edward and cancel

46

The Long-Kept Secret

her trip. France could wait for now. Her love for him took precedence over everything else in her life. She would have to wait for the late afternoon train, which meant he would arrive at Charleston several hours before her.

A surge of excitement overtook her for a few minutes. She sat on the bed, visualizing herself pursuing him and thinking how absurd she would look. What would she say to him? What would he think of her? Would he scold her for pursuing him? Fuchsia would probably lecture her about how improper it was for a woman to chase a man since it only led to losing self-respect. "Oh, Fuchsia, I hope you are right. I better not be making the biggest mistake of my life," she whispered.

She packed the sensational dress Edward had bought her, which she would adore forever. She believed they would see each other again one day. She envisioned their excursion to a faraway land, not knowing where or when, but she knew it would happen. Her stomach was upset, leaving her with a dreadful feeling of lovesickness. She drank some soda water to calm it. Eventually, it subsided temporarily. She continued to wonder about her next move. *I can't figure this out now. It will make me crazy. Maybe I'll have a solution before Friday.*

She placed a small framed picture of Edward in the middle of her packed clothing. Finally, the last unforgettable item—a drawing representing their time together at Central Park—was carefully placed at the bottom.

Chapter 7

Fuchsia left the boutique and carried two large boxes to her carriage, trying to get the attention of her driver for assistance. His lackadaisical behavior annoyed her tremendously.

"Help me with these," she said before mounting the carriage. She arranged her hair and refreshed her cosmetics, feeling rushed and excited about visiting her friend, Signora Anna and Signor Giovani Angelini, a prosperous Italian woman.

Their next stop was at the Angelini's home for a social gathering in celebration of her husband's fortieth birthday. She was expecting her at noon, but it was already half past the hour. When the carriage stopped, she could see her standing at the entrance, waving happily and pleased by her arrival. Her social circle consisted of affluent and highly educated Southerners. She had been the president of Charleston's High Society Women's Club for several years. Her involvement in the National Women's Suffrage Association, which proposed that women should have the same rights as men, brought great admiration among the community. After Fuchsia complimented her outspoken views at one of the meetings, they immediately became friends. Their friendship developed during Suzanna's three-week absence. She hoped to meet the man of her dreams at Signor and Signora Angelini's home since every well-known Charleston resident attended the celebrations.

The Long-Kept Secret

Anna greeted Fuchsia along the path that led to her home. She wore a colorful dress with long pearls that hung low and tied at the end. Her gray hair hung loosely along the sides of her face. Fuchsia could hear the pianist playing one of her favorite pieces by Mozart as she entered the hallway, and she delicately bowed her head to the other guests. Anna made a loud sound when one of her servants spilled champagne on the floor. She called out her name in Italian and told her to clean up immediately.

"Fuchsia, I have something I want to discuss last week's meeting. Come this way to meet my guests."

Several people were discussing Renaissance art and architecture. The couple had recently been to Italy and had returned with several precious pieces. Fuchsia's eyes caught Giovanni, a jolly, stocky man describing a painting to a gentleman. He pointed to specific areas along its edges with eyes filled with pride.

When Fuchsia realized their discussion was altering into an argument, she walked over to Giovanni's side to break the tension between the two gentlemen. She noticed that the hostess was too absorbed with her servants' duties even to be aware of her husband's debate over Pre-Raphaelite and Renaissance art.

The host's eyes lit up as Fuchsia approached them. "Fuchsia, I didn't see you arrive. My dear, I know how boring it can be for someone your age. You look young enough to be my daughter. Most of the guests here are old enough to be your parents. We must dance."

With a delighted acceptance, she was swept off her feet to the center of the immense parlor. People stood back and admired them. A few joined, merrily changing the atmosphere from a humdrum mood to a happy one.

Fuchsia spotted the tall gentleman who had stood by the painting. He had distinguished features and fine apparel. She pranced around the floor, smiling and laughing with her partner. His appearance elevated her spirits as they danced closer to him. Their eyes connected when they gazed at each other. Finally, Giovanni led her to the sofa.

The mysterious guest stood close by with a glass of gin.

49

Alexandra Lamour

She sat with her hands clasped in her lap, and her shoulders were perfectly straight. Her eyes twinkled as she followed the dancers' movements with contentment and pleasure. Her desire to speak to him grew when Anna invited her to have something to eat.

"Yes, in a bit. Thank you, Anna." She waited for several minutes for the unknown guest to approach her.

Suddenly, he appeared before her, slightly bowing his head. "My name is Edward. Edward O'Reilly. "You are quite the dancer. Would you care to dance, ma'am?

"Yes, thank you." She smiled kindly.

"I do hope you are enjoying yourself." He led her to the dance floor. He released her once and pulled her body toward him.

"Oh, yes, it is lovely. This is not my first time here." Anna is quite the event planner."

"And may I ask your name, fair lady?" He smiled, pleased to be dancing with the most elegant woman at the party.

"Fuchsia Montgomery." She smiled as well. She had danced with other gentlemen, but this one was different. She loved his deep voice and laughter. When he mocked the lady with the large feather hat, Fuchsia giggled coyly.

Signora Angelini complained to her husband about one of the servants and mentioned Edward O'Reilly dancing with Fuchsia.

After the dance, Edward escorted Fuchsia to the dining room table. Diverse foods were on a satin tablecloth. Bottles of Italian wines filled a smaller table against the wall. Many guests were drinking the imported wines. Several candles burned in the center of the table to give a welcoming atmosphere.

Fuchsia was smitten by Edward's charm and warmth and didn't want the day to end.

"Am I being presumptuous to request to visit you one day?" he inquired.

"Well, Mr. O'Reilly, I guess." She turned to the right and then looked directly into his eyes. "I was hoping you would." She smiled again.

The Long-Kept Secret

In the late afternoon, the majority of guests left. After Fuchsia thanked the hosts for a wonderful time, Edward walked her to the door. He watched her fancy carriage turn in a different direction from the other carriages. She was overjoyed to have met a well-mannered and distinguished man.

Chapter 8

The *Transatlantic* arrived at the Rock of Gibraltar on a cool and windy day. To the left, Suzanna could see the enormous rock towering over the crystal blue and picturesque waves of the Mediterranean. The sea was inviting and daring to travelers who embarked on its mystifying waters. She loved how the Atlantic and the Mediterranean joined as one entity, unifying the world's four corners with its gusty winds. Suzanna's head remained upright as the ship passed the vigilant rock. She was amazed by its size. Her head turned to the right to feast on Morocco's sandy beaches and the glimmering waves that drifted eastward. She could feel the hot Mediterranean sun upon her face, and the coolness of the breeze slightly chilled her body.

Marseilles was not far off the coast of Spain, which meant they would be arriving within a day. Suzanna's anticipation increased as she thought of her destination. She had enjoyed the voyage across the Atlantic, but the real excitement would be reaching the shores of Marseilles. For a fleeting moment, she recalled Edward O'Reilly and the time they had shared. She immediately became melancholy, fretting and moping bitterly and trying to force back the tears that fell from her aching eyes. She wiped off the tears and tried to convince herself that it was not over and that they would meet again under better circumstances. She had fallen deeply in love with Edward on the day they met. He had not revealed his feelings for her, but she longed to know them.

The Long-Kept Secret

"I will not cry again," she whispered to herself.

A man standing a few feet away turned toward her and said, "Such a beautiful woman to be crying on such a beautiful day." He had a strong French accent. "Why?"

Suzanna let out a laugh and smiled.

"My name is Maurice DuPont." He shook her hand.

He was very humorous, and she enjoyed his presence. He was returning to Paris after a one-year stay in America. According to him, he was a famous couturier who was expanding his clothing designs to foreign lands.

After their conversation began to diminish, Suzanna said, "I must leave you now." She turned away from him.

"Please … we must dine together, mademoiselle. You did not tell me your name."

"Suzanna Smith," she said.

"You can't leave without giving me a chance to show you a little hospitality," he said with a spark of flattery, desiring to be with this nearly flawless woman who had captivated him from first sight.

They ate in a small dining room on the upper deck near the ship's bow. The vessel was sailing much smoother than the previous week now that they were near land. Suzanna kept from drinking even though he continually offered her wine. She knew that she would become depressed about Edward. Several minutes after their meal, she decided to make her exit to get a good night's sleep before they reached Marseilles. She stood up and said, "Well, I must leave you this time."

"Not yet, my dear."

"But, Maurice, it is late." She walked to the door, shook her hair, and smoothed it down.

Maurice jumped out of his seat and followed her to her cabin. His face exhibited defeat and disappointment.

"Why are you in such a hurry?" he asked with eyes full of sadness.

"I am just tired," she said.

He reached for her hand and kissed it fervently on both sides. "Then you will see me again tomorrow before we dock."

53

Alexandra Lamour

"Of course, Maurice. Until then." She smiled and batted her long eyelashes.

The afternoon sunlight danced upon the blue waves. The wind caused Suzanna to shiver from the cool breeze as her eyes followed along the coastline of France. She scrutinized the rugged landscape and sharp, uneven mountains. The brownish-green mountains were so different from the mountains and hills in America.

"Did you sleep well?" Maurice asked.

"Very well. Thank you," she answered. "What do you want from me?"

"I don't understand what I have done to make you so angry. If it was my drinking, I apologize. If it was my bold conduct last night, I humbly apologize too." There was sincerity and humility in his voice.

"I didn't mean to be so rude," she said. "Now, didn't you say that you had some wine stored away for a chilly day?"

"*Oui*, of course," he answered.

She placed her arm through his, and they headed for the chairs on the promenade.

When news arrived that they would reach Marseilles in the evening, Suzanna had a crew member pack her baggage. She was glad the ship was docking soon, especially with a companion who would assist her during her travels through France. Since they were both heading for Paris, it would be convenient for Suzanna to have a male native as a chaperone.

Paris was a city with unique culture, art, and history. The city of her dreams was within reach. Maurice was a gentleman during their eight-day trip, and he tried day and night to win over Suzanna's obstinate heart.

They sat comfortably by the unlit fireplace in the hotel's lobby.

Maurice said, "I have not forced my way into your life or tried to persuade you to do things against your will. I only ask that you remain loyal to me as I have promised myself that I will remain loyal to you. Suzanna, I have fallen in love with you. I know that you have sensed my feelings for a long time." His face was glum.

Suzanna turned her head away, feeling a little guilty. She could not look into his eyes.

He reached for her shoulder.

Her thoughts wandered, and she felt a lump rise in her throat, which made it impossible to respond to his gentle touch. She sat still for several minutes and then rose. The past seemed to be drifting out of her reach. She did not force a smile or cover up her feelings. She was not going to allow herself to yield to him. She knew nothing about his private life. "It's late, and I'm going to bed now," she said calmly without looking into his pleading eyes.

Maurice rose from the chair and tried to embrace Suzanna.

She raised her hand and told him to stop.

He said, "I'm sorry. I would do anything for you, Suzanna. I'd forsake my present status to be with you. Anything for you … anything."

Suzanna awoke at five o'clock in the morning to get an early start. She wanted to depart before Maurice knocked on her door. She could not bear the thought of being in anyone else's arms after meeting Edward. She swiftly gathered her belongings and left for the carriage. To her disappointment, Maurice was waiting for her. She boarded without saying a word. There would be a more convenient time to separate from him once they arrived in Paris.

Joigny was one hundred kilometers from her destination, which meant they would arrive in the latter part of the afternoon. The driver was hoping to arrive before sunset. She watched the sun ascend over the green pastures and turned the sky bright orange. At noon, they had stopped at an inn for a quick lunch.

It was quite a way to Melun. Unfortunately, they would arrive after sunset. They would continue for several hours in the darkness. She felt a slight chill and covered her body with a warm blanket that the courteous driver passed to her.

Alexandra Lamour

By the time the carriage arrived in Paris, Suzanna was so exhausted that she could barely keep her eyes open. She shook herself to alter her wearied state as she stared at La Seine Riviere in the evening light. With gas-lit lamps along its borders, it was the most splendid and striking view she had ever seen. She imagined what it would have felt like to be Josephine on her way to meet Napoleon at Le Palais Royal. To the left, L'Eglise de Notre Dame stood silent along the river, concealing centuries of mystery and intrigue. It had lured pilgrims with broken hearts and prayers for God to answer; other visitors came for historical and architectural purposes. All the books she had read about Paris could never describe the scenes she saw.

The carriage stopped in front of the Grand Hotel du Louvre, which was on the river, about half a block from the palace. The driver carried her baggage to the main entrance. He made a quick bow as she placed money in his receptive hand. Then a porter carried the baggage into the main lobby. Suzanna entered the hotel alone and was relieved as she glanced back at the carriage leaving with Maurice.

Suzanna went to her suite and took a hot bath. Then she put on the dress Edward had purchased her in New York. She entered the dining room and sat at a secluded table. There were many fashionably dressed Europeans.

The stylish couple to her left was quietly discussing intimate matters. She thought about how silly she must have looked entering alone, and she tried to leave before the waiter arrived. It was too late, and he stood over her with a menu.

"Something has happened, and I must leave at once," she said.

"Oui, mademoiselle." He snapped his fingers, and the maître d' led her out.

As she walked through the main lobby, she spotted Maurice talking to the receptionist, which annoyed her.

He saw her and approached. "My dear Suzanna, why have you ignored my messages?" There was frustration on his face.

The Long-Kept Secret

"I thought it was best to go our separate ways. I do not think it would be wise for you to come to the hotel again." He was becoming more annoying by the day.

"You cannot think it is over. No!" He reached for her hand.

"It is all over? There was never anything between us. Maurice, you have let your imagination go wild. I am going to my room. I am not feeling up to discussing this any further. Good night."

The next day, Suzanna awoke to heavy knocking at the door.

Maurice wanted to share some coffee on the balcony.

She agreed and walked to the marble railing with her back to him. "I have decided you should leave. I will stay in Paris for one more day before I depart for another city."

"I don't understand. I don't know what you want out of me. You are tearing me apart. You are cutting away at my heart—slowly and painfully." He stood beside her and stared at her exquisite profile.

Her long eyelashes gracefully blinked while she gazed at the breathtaking views of the streets of Paris and the clay-tiled roofs.

A flock of birds squawked in the clear blue sky.

"There is someone else in my life," she declared, realizing he was an unstable man who had problems making decisions. It was best to get away from him—and the sooner, the better.

He was irritating her. He was no comparison to Edward; she had to listen to her heart. Edward was the only man she desired, and no other man could ever match up to him. She was pretending to leave Paris so he would not pursue her. She walked back to the salon and put on her black hat. She opened her purse to touch up her cosmetics.

Maurice remained on the balcony; his face was downcast for a while, and then he exited her room without looking at Suzanna.

The next day, Suzanna checked into Hotel Paris. It was a quaint hotel located a few minutes away. She had the hotel maid unpack for her as she sat on the balcony and enjoyed a croissant and a hot cup of coffee.

That evening, she dressed to the nines and went to the dining room for dinner. She wore a colorful floral dress, a silk sash, and a pearl necklace with matching earrings that she had purchased in

57

Alexandra Lamour

New York. She noticed a couple eating quietly in the corner. While Suzanna read the menu, the waiter asked her to join Monsieur and Madame Chevalier. They were the owners of the hotel.

"Oh, that is very kind of them." She thought it was a good idea to meet the owners and to have some company.

The couple was much older, and a young woman eating alone could reveal the wrong signal.

"I'm glad you accepted the offer," Madame Chevalier said with a British accent. "Such a lovely young lady without a companion is a shame."

Monsieur Chevalier had aristocratic features and was very skinny. He smiled. "This is my wife, Agatha. I'm Pierre."

"Suzanna Smith," she responded and shook their hands. "Thank you for inviting me to your table."

Madame Chevalier and his wife could have passed as siblings.

"We met in London on one of my business trips," Mr. Chevalier said.

"Yes, and we fell in love, got married, and have been living in Paris for the past two decades."

They ordered the special of the day and several desserts. Suzanna attempted to pay, but Madame Chevalier pushed her hand gently away.

"Miss Smith, it is our pleasure. You must come to a cancan performance before you leave Paris." She raised her cup of tea. "It is a high-energy, physically demanding dance that became popular in the 1840s."

"Oh, yes. I read about it in a French magazine back home. I would love to attend." Her eyes sparkled in the candlelight.

"I read an interesting story in *Victorian Magazine* about a lord in London. Pierre, what was his name?"

Mr. Chevalier said, "Waterford, yes. It was titled 'Lord Richard Waterford II, England's Most Sought-After Bachelor.' It was about a lord in search of a wife. There was a list of available ladies."

Suzanna listened intently as the Chevaliers spoke about the Waterford family's reputation in England and how the lord had

The Long-Kept Secret

become every available woman's desire. His dashing looks and striking personality could captivate the heart of any woman in the land.

Monsieur Chevalier said, "In his younger years, his father, Lord Bartholomew Waterford I, was an active member of the House of Lords in Parliament. For ten years, he was cabinet minister, making him one of the most reputable members in office. His work gained the family notoriety in the government and amongst the British citizens."

Madame Chevalier said, "Lord Richard II followed his father's footsteps by sustaining the family name without blemish. But, like every man, it was time for him to settle down, according to his father's wishes."

"Intriguing story," Suzanna said. She promised the Chevaliers they would meet again before her departure. She went to her room in better spirits than earlier. The Chevaliers had helped her forget about Edward temporarily.

She created an itinerary for one more week in Paris before returning to Charleston. She loved Paris and hoped to return one day—but not alone. It was a perfect place for couples in love. The *Parisian* on the coffee table had an article about the "City of Love and Romance." She looked down at a couple walking on the street and wished it was her and Edward. She wondered how a man could make her feel so happy and miserable. Love was such a complex emotion. The ache, the longing, and the wondering tore through the very core of her being. By releasing Edward from her life, she could move on, but her obstinate heart would not permit it to happen. Her love for him gave her strength, and she refused to let him go.

Chapter 9

Fuchsia sat on the stool in front of the mirror and arranged her hair in a bun. She put a tall, round hat on her head and tucked her hair under it. It didn't coordinate with her dress, and she tossed it on the bed. Nothing seemed to match her ensemble. She looked in her silver containers of cosmetics and closed them quickly when the carriage arrived. She rushed to the window, thrust her head out, and waved and shouted joyfully as the carriage stopped. It was Suzanna. Finally! She wore the latest French fashion, and her hat matched her floral dress and purse. The driver proudly held her hand as she walked down the steps of the carriage. Her laughter rang through the stillness of the morning. It was wonderful to have her sister back home.

Her sister continued to watch Suzanna from the window, and her bizarre conduct surprised her. Something had altered her personality drastically. Her confident energy transcended to Fuchsia. Her smile and bold eyes had changed in the past several weeks.

Fuchsia returned Suzanna's wave and descended the staircase. Since she was part owner of the plantation, she should have a title of importance.

Suzanna entered the hallway, dressed lavishly for traveling. Her hair was beautiful, and her makeup made her look like she was going to an important festivity. Her self-reliance had changed dramatically as she walked, poised and assertive, down the hallway.

60

The Long-Kept Secret

Fuchsia called the servants and told them to assist her with her sister's baggage. She asked for lemonade to be served in the parlor. Fuchsia had eagerly anticipated Suzanna's return after she had received the news at the hotel in New York upon her arrival from Europe. Her letter had been addressed in a fancy envelope with gold trim along the sides. The news had driven her to leave New York much earlier than planned.

Fuchsia wore a simple yellow dress, and tenderness radiated from her face. "Suzanna!" She stretched out her arms. "I am so happy to see you again! I dreamed about this reunion." She dried her eyes with a handkerchief and kissed her cheeks.

"My dear, dear sister!" exclaimed Suzanna. "I have waited so long for this moment!"

The letter had explained Suzanna's mother's death, which had been wrapped in mystery for so long. She altered the truth of her mother's African American origin, proclaiming that she was of British heritage, a sister of Miss Hathaway's, and the news of their relation was much more than she believed Suzanna could handle at one time.

"I can't believe it, Fuchsia! My father was Lord Montgomery!" She fell back into the chair.

The long, treacherous years in the orphanage seemed like an eternity. Why did she have to suffer for her parents' infidelity? Her sister could never feel the pain that she endured.

For Christmas, Suzanna had received a torn stocking, a ragged old skirt fastened with a large pin, and a baggy sweater. None of the orphans had received or exchanged gifts. The horrendous meals were always inadequate and tasteless, which caused constant hunger pains in their half-empty stomachs. The absence of basic needs and a promising future had been painfully far from her sister's reach.

"Suzanna, if I could help you forget your past, I would," she said. "If I could only help you escape from the horrible memories. I can't imagine the pain you have been carrying all these years."

Alexandra Lamour

Suzanna gazed out the terrace door window at the well-maintained garden. Greedy birds were flocking to some stale bread discarded by the cook. Fuchsia's flowers were swarming with wasps.

"Happy? How could I ever be happy? Will my past ever leave me alone?" She began to cry bitterly.

Fuchsia walked over to Suzanna and hugged her. Her heart ached for her sister's insurmountable pain. The pain was beyond understanding, and it was creeping around her like a shadow.

"Tell me everything about your trip," she said in an attempt to change the mood. "I'm interested to hear about a part of the world I have never seen."

"I had a wonderful time," she declared.

Fuchsia sat on the sofa. "Well, what was your favorite site?"

"I liked every part of the trip. Paris is incredible. It has so many sites. The train ride back was lengthy and tedious. There were few passengers with whom to converse, but no one was intriguing. It sure is nice to be home."

She rose from the sofa and located a small valise in the hallway. She pulled out a painting of a beach by a famous French artist. "I bought this for you. I hope you like it."

"It's lovely. Thank you so much."

As Fuchsia gazed at the painting, Suzanna had the urge to tell her all about Edward. She convinced herself the timing was wrong since Fuchsia looked like she had something important on her mind.

"I have some exciting news for you. I know the best has already happened for both of us. This news concerns a private matter. As you know, there comes a time when we grow weary of living alone and desire a fulfilling relationship to fill a void. The need to experience a feeling of completeness." Fuchsia cleared her throat and looked into Suzanna's big brown eyes. "I found a man who has asked me to marry him. The wedding is scheduled for next month."

"You are getting married? I don't believe it! You've just met him!"

"Suzanna, you can't disapprove of this. I know it's a surprise. When it's the right match, time does not matter."

"I don't understand. It happened so quickly."

The Long-Kept Secret

"He is the one I've been searching for," she added with twinkling eyes. "There is nothing to fear. Everything remains as I stated in the letter. You will always own 50 percent of our father's fortune. I will never take that away from you."

Suzanna's face turned ashen, but she slowly regained her natural color. "I wasn't thinking about my inheritance, Fuchsia. I trust you."

"We will continue this conversation later. Why don't you lie down? You look tired. Some rest will do you some good."

She put Suzanna's glass on the table by the luxurious sofa.

"Fuchsia, what is his name?" Her head rested on a satin pillow.

"Edward O'Reilly," she replied as she closed the door.

Suzanna was perplexed.

Chapter 10

Unaware that she had spent a few hours that night on the sofa, she vaguely recalled Fuchsia entering the parlor and trying to take her to her bedroom. She had been too tired from crying so much when she heard the startling news. She arose and thought about their conversation. "It cannot be," she whispered as she walked over to the mirror to arrange her untidy hair. She stared at herself for a long time, observing her beautiful face turning hard and angry. Her eyes burned with contempt, her strength weakened, and she could feel her life spiraling downward. Overtaken by sentiments, she analyzed her options until anger took precedence.

Feelings of hatred filled her heart. "She's not going to get away with this! I swear! How could she take away the only man I love? The only man I could ever love!" She stood with a heart of stone. Half-crazed with confusion, she wondered how they met.

Their relationship was intolerable. The agonizing nights she longed for Edward resurfaced. Their potential reunion had been snatched away. *It's unthinkable. It's all a misunderstanding.* Edward didn't look like the marrying type—and now he was marrying her sister? He was a man of the world. Settling down now appeared ridiculous. What could they have in common? She didn't seem like his kind of woman. It was a mistake! "God as my witness, the wedding will be stopped!" she exclaimed.

The Long-Kept Secret

When she calmed her nerves and thought about her encounter with Edward, she was bewildered. The experience had lingered in her mind for weeks. She looked in the mirror, mesmerized by the image of her defeated self. She held up her head with optimistic eyes. He was her answer to all of life's problems. He was all she would ever need. She would finally be with that one person who fulfilled her needs. She wondered about the possibilities before her. Once he saw her again, he would forget about Fuchsia. The thought of him coming back into her life was exhilarating. *Oh, Edward! We will be together finally!*

A servant spotted her at the door, and Suzanna ordered her to leave and do her business. She hurried up the revolving staircase to her room, attempting to conjure up a way to get Edward back. Suzanna neatly arranged her clothes in her closet, searched for cosmetics, and redid her face before changing her clothing. As she was about to exit, she heard a faint noise at the door.

She cleared her throat. "Yes?"

"It's me. Can I come in?" Fuchsia asked.

"Of course ... I was just tidying up."

"I can come back if you wish."

"Oh no, I'm almost finished." She took a deep breath, exhaled, and turned the door handle.

Fuchsia kissed her cheeks and said, "I hope you are feeling better ... more relaxed. I'm so sorry you had a tiresome trip. Please come eat. It'll be ready in about fifteen minutes."

Suzanna placed her hand on her head and replied, "So tired. I have such a headache. I think I'll pass." She forced a quick short smile and sat down near the bed. "If a servant can bring me my breakfast, I'll try to eat a bit."

"I hope my wedding plans haven't startled you."

"No, why would you say that?" She tried to remain calm.

"You seemed rather upset last night. Was it something I said?"

"Upset? You are mistaken." She tried to cover up her emotions. "It was a long trip, and I need to rest a bit today. That's all."

"If you need anything, just let me know."

65

Alexandra Lamour

Suzanna forced down the bread and eggs and nearly scorched her tongue on the coffee. She put the cup down on the saucer with a crash and spilled most of it on the tablecloth. She took her fan, waved it around her face, and thought about her plans with Edward. She decided to go to him, tell him how she felt, and perhaps win him over. It wasn't too late. There was still hope for getting him back. She left immediately for Charleston.

To her amazement, after having her driver inquire about the O'Reilly's dwelling, she discovered he lived in a large Victorian home near the theater. "Drive around the back of the house, and when you see me, return at once."

Suzanna rushed out of the carriage before the driver came to a complete stop. She lifted her long silk skirt and gracefully walked to the main door. She paused before knocking, thinking about what she would say to Edward. What would he say to her?

An old butler opened the door and gazed at her through a tiny pair of spectacles. "Yes?"

"I would like to see Mr. O'Reilly please."

"Yes, I see. And whom shall I say is calling?" He led her into the hallway.

Suzanna stopped and looked into the old man's face. "Suzanna Montgomery." She examined the house's interior and dark, heavy furniture. She knew it had to be Edward's taste since it reflected his personality. In the hallway by the stairs, she examined the painting of a man dressed in formal apparel. It was probably his father since they possessed similar physical characteristics.

When she heard Edward's footsteps growing louder, her heart filled with joy. She wanted to rush to him, but she convinced herself to hold her place. His face was different, and he looked surprised as he led her into the library.

"I had to come see you." Her face was flushed.

"I had no idea that you were related to Fuchsia. Are you truly her sister? You told me your name was Suzanna Smith. I'm still shocked by the news."

He closed the door quickly.

66

The Long-Kept Secret

"When I returned from Europe, I learned about my true heritage. We had the same father."

"It's uncanny! I learned of this recently. Fuchsia spoke of you as though you were always sisters. I thought your first name was just a coincidence." He walked about the room nervously with his hands clasped behind his back in deep thought.

"I didn't tell you that I lived outside Charleston because I didn't know your true feelings for me. When you told me you had been in the South, I had no idea you resided here. I assumed you were visiting for business." She moved closer to him to share her real feelings. "I can't believe you are planning to marry Fuchsia. Tell me it isn't true. Didn't I mean anything to you in New York? Don't I mean anything to you now? It can't be!"

"Suzanna, it's too late," he said. "A lot of things have transpired during your absence. You can't change our plans."

Suzanna thought about Fuchsia and how wrong she was for him. Perhaps he was tired of the cheap short-term relationships that temporarily satisfied him. Maybe it was over now that he had found Fuchsia. There was something different about him that she didn't like. His fun behavior in New York seemed to have vanished. He was serious and reflective. Fuchsia had changed him.

"It's time to move on. My days of recklessness are done. I'm getting older, and getting older means settling down. No more shenanigans."

Suzanna wondered about her sister's power over him. She knew Fuchsia's purity and innocence contrasted with her inferior breeding. They were two different women.

"Fuchsia's presence made me reexamine my past indiscretions. Being with her could give me a chance for a new beginning. I am ready to live a more righteous life. She is a rarity." He paced the floor and turned to look at her trembling body.

"What can I do to have you?" She reached out her hand. "I haven't been able to forget you for weeks. I know I behaved childishly our last evening, but I feared I was losing you. I dreamed about the day we would be together again."

Alexandra Lamour

He gazed at her for a while and contemplated his next move. Then he paced about the room.

"Please don't leave me!" she burst out in desperation. "We could go away. My sister will never know. Please tell me you love me." She searched his face for reassurance.

He approached her and said, "Suzanna, you are stunning. Words cannot express your unique beauty, but Fuchsia is better for me. I'm going to marry her." He headed for the door.

Suzanna was at his heels. She wanted to caress his soft golden hair. She truly believed they had been created for each other and belonged together.

"No, you don't mean that!" She reached for his hand.

Edward touched the warm tears on her face. Her sadness enhanced her beauty. In a moment of weakness, he embraced her voluptuous body and pulled it closer to him with great force. He could not resist her pleading.

His musky fragrance brought back memories and ignited Suzanna's passion for him. She had never felt such a need for any man but him. "I know you love me. I know you do, Edward." She stopped crying and laughed.

He pressed his hungry lips against her forehead and stroked her hair delicately. He wanted her one more time. Her body intensified his arousal.

"I love you more than Fuchsia ever could," she whispered. She yearned for his muscular arms that comforted her. His presence made her feel alive again. She moved toward the door, locked it, boldly slipped off her dress, and dropped it on the floor. Her lace corset accented her full bosom, slender waist, and long legs. "Edward, hold me. Please don't let me go. I'm yours forever." She undid the buttons of his shirt, kissed his lips, and pressed her body against his chest. "Make love to me like you did in New York." She forgot herself and allowed her desires to override her worries about losing him to her sister.

"Have you been intimate with Fuchsia?" she asked and quickly turned away to wait for his response.

The Long-Kept Secret

"No." He pulled her toward him and proceeded to kiss her with fervor.

She did not hold back. She knew she had the upper hand since Fuchsia's physical attributes were no competition. Their sexual chemistry was incredible.

Subdued by passion, he carried her to the velvet divan and slowly took off her corset. Then he undressed, gazing into her eyes. As he began kissing her from head to toe, she became wild for him. Her excitement intensified his uncontrollable manly desires. She could tell their longing for each other was mutual.

"Say you love me," she whispered. "I know you do. I can feel it. Edward, say it."

"Yes, I love you. I love your passion and spontaneity. Oh my God, you are so captivating." Her beauty enraptured him. He could not stop himself from continuing. "You are a treasure." He continued to kiss her face and every part of her body, allowing himself to have his way with her. She gave her total being in an attempt to win him back. Time was of the essence, and she knew she had little to spare before she lost him forever. She hoped time was on her side.

After they both reached satisfaction, she slowly rose from the divan and grabbed her corset. Then she leaned over and kissed his forehead.

They smiled at one another.

"I need to wash up."

"There's a small lavatory to the right," he stated while gathering his clothing.

As she was about to slip on her corset, he stood by her partially clothed.

"Please, don't speak unless you have something kind to say," she pleaded. "Your words have been ruthless, piercing my heart. I couldn't bear any more criticism." She placed her finger over his lips.

"I'm just admiring you."

"You can admire me for as long as you want, but you have to make a choice, Edward. Fate lies in your hands."

Suzanna's stubbornness surprised him.

He released a sigh of confusion and rubbed his face. "Yes, I am aware of the situation. The moment you walked through the door, I knew I was in a predicament."

"It's simple Edward. It's me or Fuchsia."

He washed up and continued to dress as Suzanna arranged her hair in the adjacent mirror.

He will need time to think it over. It will not be an easy decision. He is committed to my sister, she thought.

She wasn't finished with him yet. Desire took precedence over everything else. When she started to undo the gusset ties in the back of his trousers, he did not stop her.

"Are you trying to tire me out?"

"I'm making sure you have no more energy for another woman ever again."

Her sarcasm delighted him. Suzanna admired his virility and enjoyed watching him succumb to it. She slipped off her corset slowly, staring into his eyes for approval. Then she moved her firm body against his physique, taking control. She knew he could not refrain from her persistence. Power prevailed as she watched his satisfied facial expressions. She felt victorious. They enjoyed each other's bodies more the second time and rejoiced together after being fulfilled.

Suzanna knew he had never been physically delighted by another woman more than her. She saw the vulnerability in his eyes when she overpowered him. He had taught her well in New York. He was hers, and no one would dare take him from her—especially now that she had found him again. Their union reignited an inner strength to confront any obstacle. She would win in the end.

"Let's stay like this forever," she whispered in his ear as she kissed it gently. "Let's leave it to fate." She reminded him of his words. "Well, it looks like fate is in our favor. You need to marry me—not Fuchsia," she implored. "No woman could ever love you as much as I do. Not even Fuchsia."

Edward remained silent as he pondered his plight. Suzanna's presence had deeply stirred up his emotions.

The Long-Kept Secret

They sat on the couch wrapped in a large blanket. Then he poured some red wine into two long-stemmed crystal glasses. His calmness and confidence were qualities she cherished. Suzanna had planned to spend the rest of the afternoon with him and dreaded leaving. Her biggest regret was returning to the plantation. She had to keep him away from her sister as long as possible to get him back. She had to convince him they were a better match. Satisfaction overtook her as she watched him light his cigar leisurely. She loved every minute they spent together, favoring his seductive moves and laughing at his silly remarks. The old Edward came back to her. In her eyes, he was her world.

He dismissed his servant for the day and told him to return in the early evening. His driver was informed to take his message to Fuchsia concerning a business meeting. It stated it would be best to get together the following day.

When they were alone, he swooped Suzanna into his arms and carried her upstairs to his bedroom. The lush canopy bed matched the draped velvet curtains. Everything in the room reflected Edward's personality. He laid her gently on the bed and then lowered the chandelier by pulling on its chain and slowly lit each candle. Suzanna watched him move around the room and stop by the burning wood in the fireplace. He lit his cigar. Smoking was the best way to clear his thoughts. Then he turned to look at her in deep reflection.

"I can't live without you." She walked over to him and took the cigar from his hand as she led him back to the bed. "Don't think too much now. Let's enjoy each other's company."

"Suzanna, …" he couldn't finish speaking as she smothered his face with kisses.

"OK. You are right." He chuckled, enjoying her childish maneuvers.

She planned on staying with him as long as possible or maybe for good. Then she thought of Fuchsia as the key to her financial independence. She would lose her inheritance even though she was also the heiress to the Montgomery fortune. Her eyes surveyed his debonair profile as he opened the soda water bottle and filled two

Alexandra Lamour

cups. *The money will not be a concern if Edward can take care of me*, she pondered.

Edward lit candles around the bathtub, poured in a flower scent of oil, and then took off his shirt. He picked up Suzanna and gently placed her in the hot, soothing bath water. She laid against his chest and closed her eyes. Enthralled by his physique, it gave her a safe feeling. He took the sponge and rubbed her arms.

"I didn't know you liked hot baths."

"I'm a shower man," he replied. "I know you do. You had plenty of baths in New York." He grinned.

The problem with Edward was he still withheld his emotions. It made Suzanna always wonder.

"I never know what you are thinking. Tell me."

"Let's enjoy the moment," he said.

She turned to kiss him and then took the sponge to rub his shoulders and chest. Suzanna believed it was going well between them as intended. If only she had the power to erase Fuchsia from his mind forever.

"Ok. That's enough. I'm melting in here." He chuckled and got out of the tub. Suzanna soon followed and quickly dressed. Edward headed for the bed and closed his eyes.

Suzanna went into the kitchen to prepare a meal as Edward napped. She took three eggs and scrambled them in a bowl. Then she diced onions and tomatoes to saute in the greased pan over the cast-iron stove. There was a truckle of cheese that she sliced into tiny pieces. The omelet, sliced bread, and orange marmalade were placed on a large plate. Finally, she reheated the early morning coffee and placed the pot on the tray.

When Suzanna arrived at the bedroom doorway, Edward sat shirtless by the low-lit fireplace. He leisurely smoked a cigar. Her love for him grew every time she was in his presence. She could read his thoughts as he rose to meet her in the center of the room.

"Let me give you some help."

"I think you will like my cooking," she stated. "You are probably famished. I'm sure you missed breakfast as usual." She smiled.

The Long-Kept Secret

"Yes, I did. And I must say you do tire me out." He leaned over to kiss her lips. "Smells good. Thank you, it's nice to have a woman's touch in the kitchen. Ralph's cooking is bland."

She hugged him and served the hot coffee while thinking how wonderful it was to be together again. *To be with Edward for the rest of my life is all I desire,* she thought.

They ate quietly and listened to the crackling sound of the fire as her mind wrestled to find a solution. It was far more complex than she had perceived it to be.

In the early part of the evening, the knock at the door interrupted them.

"Whoever it is, tell him to go away. Tell him to come back tomorrow." She ran her hands through his thick hair and kissed him passionately, trying to tease him.

The knocking continued.

"What is it, Ralph?"

"I'm sorry to disturb you, sir, but it's your fiancée, Miss Montgomery."

Suzanna shrieked and slipped on her dress.

Edward put on his trousers and shirt while she fastened the buttons. Then he combed his hair in front of the mirror. He told Suzanna to remain in the room and closed the door. She leaned her ear close to the door to hear their conversation and peeped for a moment from the top of the stairs.

Fuchsia was prim and proper as she sat with her purse on her lap. It looked as though she had plans to go someplace. "Edward! Did I surprise you? I'm making my weekly visit to the orphanage. I would love it if you could join me. I love to read night stories to the younger children."

"Of course. my dear. Your wish is my command." He took her hand and led her to the door.

Suzanna restrained from losing control of herself. "Oh, Edward. No," she whispered in disapproval. "How could you?" When she gathered her thoughts, she blew her nose, straightened her clothes, and left the room. She felt ashamed and mortified. When Fuchsia's

73

Alexandra Lamour

carriage was gone, she exited the house. When she reached her carriage behind Edward's residence, her driver was sleeping.

"Wake up," she demanded. Suzanna felt like her life was getting out of hand so she decided to visit Claudette. "Take me to Claudette's—and you better not mention any of this to Fuchsia!"

Claudette would help her. She was always good at giving Suzanna guidance. Fortunately, Claudette kept secrets quite well.

Chapter 11

Suzanna met Claudette, a saloon owner when she was a young girl and always visited her when she was discouraged by the orphanage's living conditions. Furthermore, she showed compassion for Suzanna and other orphans by serving them warm meals in the back room of the saloon, especially during the colder months. She, too, had grown up as an orphan, which made her empathize with their many needs. Unfortunately, her charitable acts had been overlooked by others because she owned a saloon. Claudette was often sneered at by churchgoers, revealing their hypocrisy.

In the saloon, parlor music and dancing filled Suzanna's ears. Claudette's saloon was known for merriment, and it was a place to forget one's troubles. However, something depressing was drawing Suzanna to it. She entered through the back door, climbed up the dingy stairs which led to an isolated room, and knocked twice.

Claudette was going over her monthly inventory at her desk. She was always in deep thought when it came to balancing her books.

When Suzanna saw Claudette, her face lit up.

"I knew you'd be back to visit!" Claudette's bright red hair and heavy cosmetics made her recognizable in the community. Her clothing was vibrant and flashy. "What is it, dear? You are like my own daughter. Come on and tell Mama Claudette your problem." She poured a glass of brandy.

Alexandra Lamour

Suzanna swallowed a huge gulp to calm her nerves. Finally, she blurted out, "I've lost the only man I have ever loved. "Oh, Edward." She sulked. Then she rubbed her aching forehead and looked up at her friend, wishing for words of consolation.

"Love?" Claudette cackled. "Is that it? You can't be serious. What did I teach you? Have you forgotten already?" She put the bottle of brandy in a locked cupboard. "Look at you. I've never seen you act like this before. I have told you to never give away your heart. Now he has taken away your strength and has left you weak and helpless. What were you thinking? Dependence on a man will only lead to disappointments." She paused. "Control yourself. You are falling apart!"

Suzanna finished her drink and told her everything that happened, slurring her words and cursing Fuchsia's name every so often. She wanted the alcohol to make the problem go away. It usually killed the pain—at least temporarily—but this pain was not temporary. She did not know how to deal with it. Even though Suzanna knew her love for Edward was a flickering candle that would be extinguished one day, she still held onto him with all her might.

"Now, why are you angry with Fuchsia? She didn't know about your relationship with Edward. I'm sure if she did, they wouldn't be together. Honestly, you should be angry with Edward." Claudette signaled one of her helpers with the wave of her fan to leave the room. "He is taking you for a fool. And playing hanky-panky with two sisters. What a predicament!" she said in a huff. "He is burning a candle at both ends, and you and Fuchsia are the fire. On the other hand, he could be more torn up inside of himself than you are. Men have a way of concealing emotions."

"I don't know his true feelings. He hides them so well. Anyway, we were intimate again. I was overtaken by passion. I feel awful. Especially when I knew they were engaged." She buried her face in her hands.

"Life is a game of chess. Every move or decision can bring luck or misfortune. Think wisely. If Edward were available, you probably wouldn't want him as much. It's always the winning that matters

The Long-Kept Secret

most." She lit a thin cigar. "I know you, Suzanna, better than you know yourself. You don't always have to win. Just let him go. Forget him. Don't wait for Edward to make the next move. You make it."

"Let him go? Forget him?" she cried. "I don't want to."

"It would do you some good to act like the lady you have become. Remember you are a Montgomery—a name that carries a good reputation in Charleston. You deserve better."

"You don't understand how I feel. You've never been in love, Claudette." Suzanna clasped her hands and placed her elbows on the table. "I can't let him go! I just can't! I was wishing you would tell me not to let him go—and that it wasn't too late. And everything would work itself out."

"So … you want me to say what you want to hear? Is that it, Suzanna? I've lived much longer than you, and I know if you come between them, it will destroy you!"

"Is that what you think? I fell in love with him before Fuchsia. It's not right. It's not fair."

"Right? Fair? Who said that life was right or fair? Well, my dear, it isn't. And it has never been nor will it ever be."

"My love for him has already poisoned me!" declared Suzanna. "I can barely sleep or eat. If I let him go, then I have no reason to go on. There will be nothing to fight for. He makes me happy. Everyone deserves some happiness." She tried to dry her eyes with a handkerchief as she cried bitterly again. "I should have pursued him when he left New York. I knew I made a mistake. I ruined everything by going to France."

"You can't change the past. Going to France or not wouldn't change anything."

"I know we'll be together today. I just know it."

She hadn't slept a wink the previous night as she thought about her situation. She was tired and worn out. Trying to solve the problem was pointless. It was too complicated with many twists and turns. How she ended up in such a mess was beyond all reason. It required a rational mind.

Before long, she fell asleep on the sofa.

77

Alexandra Lamour

Suzanna woke up feeling crushed and humiliated. Claudette was sitting at her desk with her black inventory book. She looked at Suzanna and then resumed her work.

Suzanna didn't want Claudette to reprimand her again; she didn't mention Edward. She knew she had to figure it out on her own. She was fighting her own battle. She was fighting for love.

"Claudette, I have to return to the plantation," she remarked as she reached for her pocket mirror to reapply some smeared cosmetics.

"Do what you have to do, my dear. I truly hope it works out for your sake. You know I will always be here for you. Be careful."

Suzanna touched her shoulder with gratitude. Claudette's life experiences made her wise. She always had sound judgment. Furthermore, she was good at predicting the outcomes of relationships and business transactions.

When she returned to the plantation—where she swore she would never enter intoxicated—the alcohol had worn off. She noticed a foreign carriage on the pathway by the main door. When she got out of the carriage, she heard laughter in the house. It sounded like a social gathering. She heard Fuchsia's voice, but she did not recognize the other person's muffled speech. Could it be Edward? Were they mocking her foolish behavior? She would never permit anyone to make fun of her. Perhaps Edward had told her everything about their relationship in New York.

Suzanna glanced through the parlor doorway and found Fuchsia and Edward in each other's arms. She gasped, leaned against the wall, and prayed that they had not been alerted by her emotional outburst.

Fuchsia said, "I have invited the Charleston Charity Organization for a luncheon on Friday. I hope we will raise enough money to complete the orphanage I told you about."

"Oh, my dear, it is so rare to find such kindness."

"Oh, Edward," she whispered.

Suzanna felt nauseous and bit her gray glove to control her emotions. Gathering her strength, she walked into the room.

"Suzanna!" Fuchsia dashed to her side. "I want you to meet Edward."

The Long-Kept Secret

Suzanna reached for his hand. "Nice to meet you." Her eyes were begging him to love her instead.

Fuchsia said, "You see, Edward, I have flesh and blood. We were talking about our wedding plans. There are so many things to do."

"Yes, I'm sure," Suzanna said. "A wedding is a big step in life, and it does take a lot of preparation. It's quite a commitment."

"Oh, Suzanna," Fuchsia said. "I hope we will be as lucky to share your wedding day."

Suzanna looked at Edward's cynical expression and then at her sister. She felt an urge to scratch her sister's face like a cat. Instead, she excused herself and smiled before leaving.

Edward mentioned how nice it was to have met her sister to veil their relationship.

Suzanna rushed up the stairs, enraged far more than she had ever been. Evil thoughts took control of her, and then anger filled her mind. She wanted them both to pay for her pain. She grasped the railing at the top of the marble staircase. She felt depressed, insignificant, and unworthy. Darkness was enclosing her, and she was terrified that subjecting herself to an evil spirit could be dangerous. She grabbed the railing again and stopped for a moment. Her head was throbbing. She didn't know what to do next. She bit her upper lip until it bled as she thought of their recent encounter, *I feel used and betrayed.*

On the following Friday, Fuchsia fluttered around the estate, welcomed guests into the parlor, and encouraged them to donate substantially to the charity organization she had founded a little more than three years prior. "Suzanna, I want you to meet some of my friends. We are doing another charity luncheon for the new orphanage."

Suzanna shook hands with strangers and gently kissed her close friends' cheeks as they entered the estate. They went into the parlor for tea. Her lack of enthusiasm was apparent to Fuchsia.

Alexandra Lamour

"Suzanna. I hope you can show some delight. I started this because of you. I would hate to see other orphans mistreated in any way."

"I apologize for my behavior, but I haven't been feeling well since I got back from New York."

"You better go rest. I'll be fine on my own."

"No, I'm fine. It's just a lack of sleep ... nothing else."

Fuchsia's warmth and compassion were always immediately felt among people, which gave them a feeling of being truly welcomed whenever they visited her. She had a spotless reputation in Charleston, and she was looked up to and admired more than any other woman her age. Her main concerns were the welfare of ill and poverty-stricken people.

At the end of the luncheon, Fuchsia stood up and said, "I am pleased to say today was most beneficial. Ladies, we have raised nearly eighty-five dollars, the most since the organization's opening."

Susanna stood by her sister for support. She needed to gain more attention and respect from Fuchsia's circle of friends since they were sisters now.

There was a round of applause as the guests smiled and conversed about the funds that had been donated. The people gradually parted, and by midafternoon, everyone had left except for the pastor. He continued to drink water and wipe his brow with the back of his hand.

Fuchsia approached him and smiled. "Hello."

The pastor reached for the water glass again and pushed up his glasses, slightly covering the prominent scar above his left eyebrow. He chuckled and said, "My dear, you have so much love in your heart. May God always bless you. Your devotion to your work has greatly touched the community. If there were only a handful of people of your kind, I'd be out of business. Your wedding day is approaching soon, and I'm sure you are almost prepared."

"Almost. Thank you for attending the charity drive." She noticed Suzanna wandering in the garden.

The pastor said, "I would like to share something, my dear, about the wedding."

The Long-Kept Secret

Suzanna walked into the room and sat next to Fuchsia.

The pastor excused himself.

Fuchsia said, "I hope I see him again soon."

"Perhaps," Suzanna said.

"Suzanna, you seem to be in another world. I want to talk to you about the wedding. Your gown is in your bedroom. I hope you will be pleased with it. Try it on later."

Suzanna said, "But how on earth was it finished so quickly? I didn't realize your couturier was so efficient."

"It was a favor," she responded as she called for a servant's assistance. "You need to see my wedding gown."

Fuchsia smiled and cleared her throat. "What do you think of the pearls?" She ran her fingers over the pearls on the neckline and the cuffs. "I think you'll love it once I try it on. Florence, help me take this up to my room so that I can put it on for Suzanna." She waltzed out of the room.

Fuchsia returned in the gown and turned around so Suzanna could get a good look. It was as white as snow with the finest pearls and lace.

An older servant carried her trail and bowed.

Suzanna said, "My dear sister, it is too showy! It is much too dramatic—or should I say *theatrical*. If I were you, I'd wear a more modest dress; simple is the word. Look here, Fuchsia." She moved her fingers along the dress. "All I see are pearls and lace—and the trail is far too long."

Fuchsia became pale, and her eyes widened. "I didn't realize it was so overpowering. I think Edward better look at it before I make any alterations."

"Oh, heavens no! The groom is never supposed to see the wedding gown. It is a bad omen. I know what looks best on you. First, we should go into the city and look around for some novel ideas, and then we can have your couturier make you another one."

"Suzanna, do you not realize the wedding is only two weeks away? He could never get the material in time! He is such a fidgety person who despises last-minute requests." She leaned back on the sofa.

"Well, have him shorten the trail and remove the pearls."

"Are you sure that it will look better?"

"Of course. If he cuts off the trail about here and removes these pearls, you'll be able to appreciate the flattering material."

Fuchsia was speechless as she thought about her sister's comments.

Suzanna went to her bedroom feeling somewhat victorious. Her gown hung in the closet. She angrily tore it off the hanger and threw it on her bed. It took her several minutes before she could control her emotions. When she finally had power over her feelings, she retrieved the threatening gown that reminded her of a day she prayed would never come. *I will have to work fast—or Edward will never be mine. I won't be able to live here anymore if I can't stop the wedding,* she believed.

A knock on the door announced that the couturier had been sent for and would arrive soon.

She took Edward's picture from her dress pocket and kissed it several times before putting it back in a concealed place. She applied her favorite perfume and fixed her cosmetics before going downstairs. As she reached the bottom step, she decided to get some fresh air in the garden.

Fuchsia should be able to handle it on her own and doesn't need me, she thought. When she reentered the house, she was surprised that the couturier was still there. She aimed to avoid them in the parlor, but Fuchsia invited her to join them.

Suzanna's entrance into the parlor enchanted the well-dressed man whose bows pleased her. He was rather handsome, and she was happy to have joined them. He had wavy hair, dark eyes, and olive skin. His broad shoulders and large hands reflected a trained laborer—not a man of fashion.

The Long-Kept Secret

"Have you been designing long?" Suzanna asked.

"Oh yes," he replied. "I began young, but I did not go into the fashion world until recently. My brother Maurice, who moved to Charleston with his family, was my devoted mentor."

"Maurice? What is your surname?"

"DuPont," he answered.

Suzanna felt a lump in her throat. Something made her believe that Maurice had followed her to Charleston. She had to avoid running into him because he was obsessed with her.

Chapter 12

Later that afternoon, Suzanna left for Charleston.

She went by carriage to see if it was the same man she had met on her trip. She had her driver inquire about Maurice's shop. She knew how to find it. After a conversation with a pedestrian, she spotted the shop. Since it was in the city's heart, locating it would be easy. Its exterior was in poor condition, but when she peeked inside, the quaint French shop was immaculate. She lowered her hat to one side and pretended to look at the designs in the window. A couple of women conversed with a plump middle-aged worker in a plain dress and a ragged shawl. Trying to convince herself that it was all a coincidence, she entered the store and continued to look around.

The two women were bickering about the material's color. The woman stood by patiently, barely glancing at Suzanna. She heard Maurice's voice in the back of the store calling the lady by her name, Margaret.

Suzanna turned around and left, glancing back into the window as she left. Seeing Maurice was making her irritable. It could get very complicated. It gave her great relief that she had not relinquished herself to him in a moment of weakness.

The Long-Kept Secret

Maurice wondered what was taking his brother so long at the Montgomery plantation. When Jean Claude finally arrived, the two brothers went to a cafe across the street from his shop.

"Did you see her?" he asked, shaking as he sipped his coffee.

"Oh, yes. She is not your type. She is from a different social level. You are wasting your time."

"Stop!" She had driven him to Charleston. He felt a momentary anguish soar through his soul, realizing his uncontrollable desire for her. His heart could not find inner tranquility, and he knew it probably never would. Conquering Suzanna was the greatest challenge of his life. He believed he would go mad if he failed.

"I will return the wedding gown to Ms Montgmery when I have finished the alterations." He lit his cigar.

Maurice said, "You will not return the dress. Margaret will. I hope you didn't give yourself away."

"Oh no, my dear brother. I did as I planned," he responded.

"And you, my dear brother, it would help if you learned a little from me," said Maurice.

"I think she is perfect for me." Jean Claude laughed.

"If you lay one hand on her, I will kill you!"

"Come, come, Maurice. You are overreacting."

"Scoundrel. Jean Claude." His face was as red as a beet. "Please … you do not know what you are saying. You have to promise me this will never happen, my dear brother. I have raised you from a little boy. Please don't tease me so."

Maurice was six inches shorter than his brother. The two men looked so different that it was difficult to convince anyone they were flesh and blood.

85

Chapter 13

The servants hurried to and fro, attempting to prepare for the long-awaited day.

Suzanna's lack of concern for her sister's wedding was quite evident.

Finally, Pastor Johnson, a new pastor in Charleston, appeared at the door. "And so the day has finally arrived. I'm so happy for your sister. They make such a fine couple."

Suzanna continued walking to the salon to get her shawl. Before leaving, she saw Fuchsia and the pastor talking.

She drove the carriage to Edward's residence. It was half past ten. Time was running out to convince Edward that he was making a big mistake. She was relieved to see that his carriage was still present. She lifted her head as she walked up the stairs to the main door. Three brisk knocks echoed throughout the dwelling as she fiddled with her white gloves, trying to look coy and refined. She thought her heart would explode in her chest, and she toyed with her curls.

The door opened, and Edward was alone. He was dressed poshly in preparation for his wedding and surprised to see her.

She grabbed his hand awkwardly and fumbled her way into the parlor. "Please listen to me. You are making a mistake if you marry Fuchsia."

"Suzanna, you should not have come here. It was careless of you. The wedding is today."

The Long-Kept Secret

"Oh, Edward! I love you so much!"

"Be strong." He grasped her hands. His eyes were firm and spiteful, and he turned toward the fireplace. His words struck her like the cracking sound of a horse's whip. "You do not understand, Suzanna. You are a flower blooming in the sunshine that needs to be watered and nurtured by a certain kind of man. You are blinded by love. He paced back and forth.

"Stop!" She placed her white gloves over her ears. "No, you don't mean it. I know you love me. I can see it in your eyes. You are pushing me aside in an attempt to forget our relationship entirely. Well, it happened in New York and here again. Whatever decision you make, I will always be in your memories."

She forced him to face her. "If you tell me you don't love me, I'll never bother you. I'll go so far away that you'll never see me again." She gazed into his distant eyes. "Edward, my biggest fear is walking out of this room and never feeling again what I feel when I'm with you."

His silence spoke for itself since he had already made up his mind. He looked at her and stated, "Goodbye, Suzanna."

"So is that it? I wasted all these weeks dreaming of a reunion. And now you push me aside with no feelings. I gave myself to you." She paused, shaking nervously, and declared, "You knew all along we would never be together!"

Edward had a shocked expression since he had not anticipated such an outburst. He did not budge and said again, "Goodbye, Suzanna." His tone was direct and painful. Then he departed the parlor.

As she exited Edward's residence, she felt despondent beyond belief. Overcome by anguish, she mounted the carriage. She knew it was over. Letting out a profound sigh, she rode on, allowing her emotions to override her. She tried to believe he was a horrendous person—and she was under a love spell in an attempt to forget him once and for all. The sun was laughing at her plight and delighting in Edward's final words. *Fuchsia has indeed won!*

87

Alexandra Lamour

Over the hills and down narrow, bumpy roads, she traveled past Mr. Wilkinson. He was conversing with some acquaintances and attempting to acknowledge her.

The carriage almost overturned as it traveled with such incredible velocity. She could not accept the fact that it was over with Edward. The marriage was soon. She snapped back to reality. She had no other recourse than to reveal the truth about Edward. It was necessary to hurry home. It was the only way to stop the wedding. He did not deserve her sister. Suddenly, she feared the consequences would be even more devastating, forcing her to lose the love and trust of her sister. Furthermore, Edward would probably disappear forever— never to be seen or heard of again, which would be unbearable.

On her way back to the plantation, guests traveled by carriage to the wedding. The carriage was mediocre, nothing ornate, but its occupants were lavishly groomed. The women wore exquisite gowns and hairstyles that competed with the county's finest and rarest Southern belles. People came from all over town—from all walks of life, many old friends and some new ones. Others kept busy with their work as the people gossiped. Suzanna knew it was the talk of the town. There was talk that the town's controversial mayor had been given a cordial invitation and was bringing along an unknown special guest.

The field workers who had stood by Fuchsia during the war— people whose hands toiled in the soil from sunrise to sunset to bring forth food—traveled along the dirt road. The workers were proud to be part of the celebration. They walked in their best clothing and traveled in old carts and wagons with ironed white shirts and pants and humble with cheerful smiles. The estate's grandeur and magnificence humbly beckoned all its guests, from poor to rich, to enter through its sturdy Roman columns, which appeared like soldiers guarding a fortress.

By the time Suzanna reached home, there were several carriages stationed along the entrance of the estate. She dashed into her bedroom and changed for the wedding, putting on her corset with the finest French lace from Paris. She needed help fastening the buttons

The Long-Kept Secret

along the back, which were impossible to reach. Also, the tangled underskirt around her waist was frustrating.

She called Lily. "I need your assistance with my gown."

"Yes, ma'am," she responded. "My, it is so beautiful."

"Thank you, Lily."

Suzanna turned in front of the mirror, allowing her gold satin gown to give a swift, sweeping sound as it rubbed against the wooden floor. The gown's color impeccably matched her necklace and shoes. She placed a fake smile upon her face, toyed with her beautiful curls, and walked out of the room in the most dignified fashion, knowing she had to be resilient.

She took her elegant walk down the circular staircase in an original style that almost made her look like the bride-to-be. She felt eyes following her every move, wondering how God could create such a perfect creature. She was flawless in every way. She was proud of her curves, which accented her slender waistline, and she was extra careful to move her long arms gracefully.

The guests were escorted to their seats in the garden. It was a superb, sunny day. The pastor stood at the podium with a black Bible against his chest. The pianist began as Suzanna, her maid of honor, commenced her march down the aisle. Her hands held a bouquet that coordinated with the arrangements on both sides of the aisles. Edward's back was facing her, and she wished he would make just a little sign of recognition, but he did not.

And then she came, smiling with such reassurance that not one soul would have questioned her about her choice. Her black hair hung loosely in curls with gardenias entwined throughout it. Two bridesmaids from the charity organization marched behind her with refined expressions on their faces as they held her exquisite gown's trail. Fuchsia's eyes gazed at her as she approached Edward's side.

Suzanna's heart pounded like heavy rain on a tin roof. She wanted to stop the pastor from proceeding, but she couldn't find the right words. *I'm trapped, doomed!* she thought. *There is no solution!*

The pastor said, "Dearly beloved, we are gathered here, in the presence of Almighty God, to unite this man and this woman. Holy

Alexandra Lamour

matrimony is a sacred act honored by God and created as a lifelong commitment to one another. And if anyone here finds cause for these two people not to be united, speak now or forever hold your peace, so help you, God.

The pastor read one of John Donne's love poems.

Suzanna began to lose awareness of her surroundings; her mind drifted in and out while reminiscing about their recent time together and their stay in New York. The drop of the glove to the romantic events they shared filled her mind with sadness. Memories of the past and present were destroyed. She felt her body begin to sway, and she believed she might faint. Her heart called out to him to stop yearning for his love. However, she did not have the strength to prevent the wedding. When she couldn't bear it any longer, she focused her eyes downward.

"And you, Fuchsia, do you take this man to be your husband, to love and to cherish through sickness and health until death do you part?"

"Yes, I do," she answered.

The pastor repeated the same words and turned to Edward. When he paused for a second, a glimmer of hope filled Suzanna's soul. It faded when he said yes.

Suzanna's heart broke, and on that day, she promised she would never fall in love again. It was unbearable to endure, and it struck her heart and soul beyond conception. Life on the plantation would be impossible to withstand. And yet, she was a half-owner, with equal rights, if not more, than Edward.

PART III

Chapter 14

1870

Just over two years after Edward's and Fuchsia's marriage, scarlet fever spread among Charleston. Edward was devastated when Fuchsia became infected with the deadly disease. The orphanage that Fuchsia visited daily carried the illness for several weeks and spread it to the townspeople. Businesses took significant losses, which caused an economic decline. They closed early daily to prevent contracting the ailment from customers. Severe cases were among children, expecting women, and poor people.

The outbreak involved a throat infection that produced a rash, fever, loss of appetite, and vomiting. Suzanna immediately reported Fuchsia's complaints of swollen glands in her abdomen to Dr. Cartwright. Red dots appeared on her face, and then a rash started on her chest and neck, eventually spreading to her entire body. Her mouth remained pale in contrast to the rest of her face.

Fuchsia asked Edward to refrain from coming into contact with her, and Suzanna's compassion for him grew even more. Employees were not permitted to enter her bedroom to prevent further spread of the disease. Instead, an old nurse stayed by her side and watched over her like a hawk with gentle eyes. The nurse was plump and wrinkled, but her hands were masculine and rough. She had worked with compassion and expertise with the wounded and dying during the

Alexandra Lamour

Civil War. Her safety was never an issue since she feared nothing—not even death.

Fuchsia spent several delirious nights with insurmountable fevers and chills. Suzanna often heard her sister calling her name and Edward's. Occasionally, she overheard Fuchsia begging God to spare her life.

Suzanna made plans to relocate to a distant part of the country. When Fuchsia discovered she was with child and infected with the illness, she canceled her plans. She discovered the dire need of her presence during her sister's ailment.

Dr. Cartwright had shared the tragic news one bleak morning. "Suzanna, your sister has little hope of surviving." He packed his stethoscope in his leather bag.

"Doctor, is there anything else that you can do to save her life?"

"No, there is nothing else I can do. The deadly disease has taken a course for the worse."

Suzanna knew that she could not desert her sister. Furthermore, her feelings of love for Edward were still present despite everything. She felt there was still hope. If God knew of her passion for him, there would be a chance for them. Her mind continued to speculate about the wonder and miracle of the universe. She continued to aspire for the grandest wish of all: the miracle of becoming Edward's wife. A refreshing burst of energy soared within her as she contemplated the possibility. Perhaps fate had taken a new direction to bring them together at last.

Suzanna kept busy during Fuchsia's illness. She heard the whispers about her sister's failing health. Even during her illness, she could still draw people's attention. Many telegrams and personal wishes were sent to their home, stressing the grief and burden felt within the community. Many prayers were sent to heaven from their local church for a recovery.

Maurice's wife, Margaret, appeared at the door, and Suzanna tried to be the best hostess, which was difficult due to the circumstances. Margaret was five feet tall, her body was round, and her skin was coarse and wrinkled.

The Long-Kept Secret

"I hope Madame Fuchsia likes the soup. My hands made her wedding dress. To think that such a lovely lady has to endure so much agony."

They sat in silence until the doctor arrived. Mrs. DuPont left quickly after.

In the library, Edward was hollering at one of the servants about medical supplies that still hadn't arrived.

Suzanna went to the door. "I overheard you; the supplies will be here shortly." She started to close the door. "I know how difficult this is for you. To have your wife and child clinging onto life."

"Suzanna, our child died last night. And now to watch the only woman I have ever loved snatched from me as well is beyond reason."

His face was unshaven, and his hair was uncombed. His eyes were bloodshot. He looked at her vulnerably. His weakness made her feel strong, and she wanted to rush to his side, but she could not. His love for Fuchsia stopped her. He began to cry, and for the first time, she saw a different side of him. He wasn't supposed to cry; he was Suzanna's fortress, strength, and rock. And was his love for Fuchsia so great that it caused him to crumble?

The doctor shouted for them to come at once.

Suzanna tried to keep up with Edward as they ascended the staircase. The bedroom door closed and was locked before she arrived. She wouldn't be able to say goodbye to Fuchsia. Was God punishing her? Maybe she had caused the death since she had longed for Edward so much. *Oh, you fool,* she thought. *You too shall crumble like Edward. You will also go mad.*

The doctor was taking so long. He told Edward to get a grip on himself. Then the wailing began.

Suzanna pounded on the door, but no one answered. "Open the door. Please unlock the door. Edward, Dr. Cartwright, I need to come in."

The door opened slowly, inviting her to see the mystery of death.

Edward was on his knees, holding Fuchsia's hand against his cheek, and the nurse stared out the window. Dr. Cartwright was looking down.

Alexandra Lamour

Suzanna approached the bed. Fuchsia's face was glowing and relaxed as though she were finally at peace. Her face was saint-like. Edward stopped crying and remained on his knees, still holding her hand. She feared that he was going to scold her or say something awful to her. Maybe he knew that she wanted her sister dead all along. Suzanna raced to the other side of the bed. "Fuchsia, I am so sorry. I was never the kind of sister I should have been," she whispered.

Edward didn't budge, and he was still holding Fuchsia's hand. His silence terrified Suzanna, and he didn't even acknowledge her presence. He appeared to have drifted into another world—a world that was so far out of Suzanna's reach. His distraught expression made her realize she would be left alone to grieve. The unbearable stillness that filled the room petrified her.

Fuchsia's death enveloped the house with an emptiness never to be filled. She was the embodiment of the plantation.

Chapter 15

The following day, Suzanna notified the pastor concerning arrangements for the funeral. Finally, she had better control of her emotions and had Edward's permission to take charge of the funeral plans. Fuchsia would lay to rest beside her parents.

Suzanna wanted a drink to calm her nerves, but she decided it might interfere with her decision-making. She needed to look over some papers in the library before she proceeded with the funeral plans. She was surprised to discover that Edward was in the library, pacing and jotting down notes at the desk.

"Good morning," she said as she approached him. "I need to get some papers from the desk."

"Excuse me. I wanted to thank you for doing this for me. I can't think straight. I find it too difficult to handle. I can't believe she is dead."

"I understand. You don't have to explain yourself. It's not a time to justify your behavior. Everyone has been grieving terribly." Suzanna took a deep breath and added, "It's not the same without her."

Edward's nicely groomed hair reflected his old self. His clean appearance offset past memories. There were several gray hairs along the side of his face. Fuchsia's death had taken a toll on him. She assumed he hadn't slept much. He was slurring his words, and he spoke in incomplete sentences.

Alexandra Lamour

When Edward left the house, Suzanna dashed to the window and watched him ascend his carriage. The driver shook the reins, and they departed. Regardless, she still loved him *dearly*. It was an inappropriate time to think of him; the funeral needed all of her attention.

She planned the funeral on Thursday if she could get everything done by then. The vast number of people was a concern. She would need her entire staff and additional workers to cater to everyone's needs.

She took the key out of the bottom drawer and walked over to the small bookcase that hid a security box. She opened the box, and her eyes widened. To her amazement, Fuchsia had slightly changed her will. Edward would receive 10 percent. The orphanage was at the top of the list. The College of Charleston's amount was in the middle—along with her staff's inheritance. She must have known that Suzanna would eventually sell and move on, and she wanted to ensure everyone close to her was part of the will.

Her eyes wandered back to the first line, which stated the provisions made in the case of her child's death. The date had coincided with the news of her expecting. She was curious whether Edward knew about the will or if she had kept it a secret. Suzanna would receive the portion promised by Fuchsia.

Even though Suzanna was a wealthy woman, a feeling of abandonment crept about her. It was her constant shadow, giving her an insecure feeling that she could not escape. She had trouble pinpointing it since her mind was on the funeral and her decision to relocate to New York. She thought of Edward and wondered how long it would take before he moved back to the city. Whenever she thought of him, her sadness vanished.

A galloping horse drew her attention to the window. She watched the stranger dismount his horse, remove his hat, and ascend the steps.

Lily knocked at the library door and whispered, "It's Mr. Irving, ma'am. He needs to speak with you."

It would take little time to sell the plantation, and there was talk that a wealthy businessman from the North, Andrew Irving, was

The Long-Kept Secret

interested in purchasing it. He had already bought Mrs. O'Connor's land and wanted to continue investing westward. After the funeral, Suzanna planned on contacting him. She looked down at the piece of paper with his name and address at the bottom of the note. "Have him come into the library."

Lily led Mr. Irving to the library.

"Please sit down."

"My name is Andrew Irving, Miss Montgomery," he declared and bowed his head while removing his hat.

"Yes, how can I help you, Sir?"

She knew he was there on business, and nobody could outsmart her in any business transaction. She wanted every penny out of him. Her sister had trained her well in the negotiating process, from exchanging information, most importantly, bargaining face-to-face. These steps helped to increase the plantation's profits. Fuchsia had inherited her father's expert business skills and believed profits were higher every year because of Suzanna's persistence.

"The property's value has increased since the end of the war. The great demand for tobacco has caused me to double the number of employees in the past few years. It has been almost impossible to keep up with the demands." She piled a bunch of papers on her desk and glanced at Irving, proud of her knack for business.

Mr. Irving rose from the sofa, approached her desk, and rested his hands on its edges. His eyes looked greedy.

Suzanna smelled tobacco on his breath, and she leaned back in her chair.

He stood upright, reached for a little metal case, and revealed several rolled-up cigars and a few slim cigarettes.

Her eyes flashed over to the box and then up to his face. "Might I be too bold in asking you, sir, to stop beating around the bush? Please get to the point."

"I plan on doing that right now, ma'am. This industry, I guarantee, will flourish even more. These fine rolled cigarettes will probably take the nation by storm." He pulled one out of his pocket and handed it to Suzanna.

99

Alexandra Lamour

She held it and twirled it in her fingers.

"How does that feel? Put it to your lips and taste it."

She passed it back to him.

"Interesting, I must say. Is it economical?"

"Absolutely."

Then she told him how much she loathed the taste as he placed the case back in his side pocket and awkwardly looked at her.

"Mr. Irving, my father, Jonathan Montgomery, immigrated to America in the late 1840s. His vision to invest in tobacco surpassed his dreams."

His chuckle caused a relaxed atmosphere in the room, and they both sat in contemplation. Finally, he pulled out his gold watch from his side pocket, glimpsed at the time, and scratched the side of his head. "What's the price?"

"What is your offer?" she responded. She wanted to maintain control of the conversation. Her lips were tight and as straight as a line. She wanted a reasonable amount. She had gone over the monthly profit report the night before and was tallying up some numbers in her mind. She thought of Abe, the overseer of the field workers. He was concerned about black root rot, and a large part of the southeastern acre had become contaminated. He had brought it to her attention that morning. It would take a year to rejuvenate that part of the crop. It wasn't the first time she had seen black root rot. She remembered Fuchsia's calm manner since she supported their father's belief in nature's renewal process. It just took a lot of time and care to see it through. Suzanna smiled when she thought of her sister's nickname, the Deal Maker, which used to make them laugh together.

Edward entered the house.

Suzanna said, "Perhaps you should come back another time. Maybe you didn't hear about my sister's recent death, and I'm much too absorbed in preparing for her funeral tomorrow."

"I'm very sorry." Mr. Irving headed for the door.

Suzanna followed Edward upstairs; she could tell he was planning to move some of his belongings back to the city. Without Fuchsia, the need to stay on the plantation was gone. It brought him misery.

The Long-Kept Secret

She caught up to him in the hallway outside his bedroom and touched his shoulder.

He turned in alarm. His eyes were empty, and his face appeared tormented.

"What are you doing, Edward?"

"There is no reason for me to remain here any longer. I'll have everything gone by the morning."

He was the only reason for her to keep the plantation, and she knew this was her last chance to win him over. Rapid thoughts flowed through her mind; she had to say something that would change his mind. A feeling of defeat overcame her again; it was the same sense of rejection that confronted her whenever she thought of losing him forever.

He entered the bedroom and left the door partially open.

"We need to talk, Edward," she said as she closed the door.

He started packing his clothes and looked out the window. She felt safe in his presence. She could tell that nothing was going to change his mind. He always made quick decisions with no regrets.

He took a final look into her eyes. "I don't understand you. I told you that we could never be together. My love for Fuchsia will never die!"

When he departed, Suzanna leaned against the wall. *Yes, it is over—for good!* His love for Fuchsia was too powerful for her to challenge! Not even death could sever their connection. It was far beyond the physical realm; it was spiritual. It transcended into another world. She knew she had to accept Mr. Irving's offer. The sooner, the better. *I've got to get away from here,* she pondered. She wrote a message to Mr. Irving. Then she asked her driver to deliver it. Later, she waited for the pastor in the library.

At half past one, Suzanna heard a knock at the main door. She had been filing some old papers. When the pastor appeared before her in the hallway, she was pleased. The former pastor had relocated to the North to seek a better life for his family.

The new pastor had been able to cause people to flock to his Sunday services like no other pastor. She had heard from city

101

Alexandra Lamour

folk that his sermons were more enlightening and inspiring to his congregation. He had invited the most despicable and immoral city people to his church, which drew more attention to him.

To Suzanna's amazement, one of them was Claudette—and she brought along some of her employees from the saloon. On Sundays, the church was packed—even though this had stirred up much older and more traditional members. He became known as the pastor of a new tomorrow, and he preached with great zeal the importance of reaching people from every walk of life.

They went over the agenda for the funeral and parted with a mutual feeling of respect. It was the first time that a preacher had moved Suzanna.

The following day was the most dreaded day of all for Suzanna. People arrived as early as eight in the morning. Since the numbers surpassed her expectations, Fuchsia's coffin would lay in the garden.

A group from the orphanage wanted to pay their respects to such a kind and generous woman. Some students from the College of Charleston wanted to show gratitude for the gracious woman who had made their education possible.

When Suzanna entered the kitchen, many staff members released their emotions by wailing for the woman who had treated them with dignity and compassion. They were grateful for the funds they would inherit.

Suzanna saw Edward conversing with an elderly couple in the garden. He looked much better than the previous day. His face had more life.

The pastor told her they needed to begin the service. If they waited for every mourner to attend, he wouldn't be able to start before nightfall. Suzanna told him to proceed immediately.

After the funeral, Suzanna saw Edward conversing with the pastor. She was about to turn away from him when he called to her. It was so pleasant to hear her name coming from his lips. It was as sweet as nature's sounds in the early morning.

"Yes?"

"I need to speak with you privately."

The Long-Kept Secret

"Of course. Let's go inside."

In the library, Edward closed the door slowly and said, "I heard you are planning to sell the plantation. I know how much it would break your sister's heart if she knew your intention. Suzanna, this is all she had to keep her going during and after the war. It was all she knew since she was a child. This land is a representation of her life. Think of the people who will be affected by your decision. Please think it over."

Suzanna's irritation reached a boiling point. He had aggravated her enough over the years. She wasn't going to subject herself to any more misery. She would tell him what was on her mind. Her blood became hot, and her eyes widened with the resentment she had always stopped from showing him. "I am so tired of how you perceive this world with your philosophical beliefs—and never once have you taken the time to see how I feel. I was in love with you, Edward. To my misfortune, you never loved me back. Only once did you tell me you loved me, but that was in a moment of passion. You made me feel small and insignificant and ache inside. I would go over details, trying to figure out what I did wrong and to convince myself it would eventually work out for us. I kept thinking I was happy to be around you and that you would someday realize you *did* love me. Crazy, isn't it?" Suzanna sat down by the window. "And when Fuchsia died, I believed this was our chance to be together. But your feelings for her were perfect in every way and were no match for me. I idolized you. This is the most dangerous love anyone can ever experience."

Edward moved closer and listened.

"You made me feel so unworthy of your love. It was never reciprocal. It's the worst feeling I have ever experienced. As insane as it sounds, I think I loved you more than Fuchsia loved you." She paused and laughed at life's irony. "No woman will ever love you the way that I did. I've lost many good years just hoping and waiting—and for what? I've been a fool. Yes, a fool for love. And what have I gained in the end? Absolutely nothing!"

Edward wanted to speak, but he allowed her to proceed.

Alexandra Lamour

"I deserve to be with someone who appreciates me and loves me. It is my chance to start over and finally put the pieces of a broken heart together. And what you think and feel doesn't matter to me anymore because I am moving forward. The plantation's sale will be by the end of the month."

She left him in good spirits, feeling better than she had ever felt in a long time. She had finally stood up to the only man she had ever loved. *Maybe he will have some respect for me now*, she wondered.

"Suzanna!" he hollered.

She refused to respond.

He had revealed a new side of himself, and it was a side she loathed. She was as tired of Edward as she was of life on the plantation. It was time to make a change. It was time for a new beginning. A new beginning made things better. Closing the old chapter in her life gave her a feeling of self-worth. Suzanna desperately hoped moving as far away as possible would help her forget him once and for all.

Chapter 16

The plantation was sold by the end of the month, just as planned. Mr. Irving's offer was more than expected. Suzanna sold off the furniture except for a few pieces she treasured. They were sent up to New York by train.

Mr. Irving's wife had adored the home when she stepped into it. She made her husband purchase every piece of furniture, including all the paintings, ceramics, and porcelain ornaments. They were some of the best items found in the South. Her arrogant gestures and rude comments caused Suzanna to mock her privately. Lily referred to her as the Yankee who had come to take over the plantation only to stir up havoc like a queen bee in a hive. Most of the help left when they discovered who their new employers were. Only a couple stayed on.

Mrs. Irving fluttered around the house, bragging about possessing the grandest estate in the South and how envious her family and friends would be once they feasted their eyes on it. Their sons were unruly and disrespectful. Lily referred to them as "lazy mules" who spent most of their time bickering over mindless issues.

Suzanna was relieved to get away from the new owners and the plantation. Her eyes gazed back at the estate as they drove away. It looked picture-perfect as it slowly diminished in size; the greenery was what she would remember the most. By the time they reached the train station, so many people were waiting to board that she lost

Alexandra Lamour

sight of Lily. When the train came to a stop, the chaos reminded her of the time after the war ended. The mass confusion put her on edge.

An irresistible tranquility came upon them as they sat in the cushioned red velvet seats. Their compartment secluded the rest of the passengers. As the train traveled through different parts of the countryside, the scenery appeared like flashes of a dream.

Her past seemed to dissipate as they traveled through North Carolina. The change of scenery opened her mind to adventure. By the time they reached Baltimore, they were exhausted. Suzanna told Lily about her plans for their stay in a Manhattan apartment.

Lily was looking forward to a new life in a big city. She had always dreamed about the North as an adventurous place. She hoped to be treated well by the Northerners.

"Lily, I know life will be better for us."

"I have been praying that when I have children, they will not go through some of the hardships I've endured as a servant."

"I know you, Lily. I'm sure you will work very hard to make their lives better—even if it means working yourself to the bone."

A short silence fell upon the train as passengers disembarked, and then it resumed motion. A delightful employee served them tea and sweets on a rolling cart.

Suzanna skimmed the *New York Times* and found an article about the enormous influx of European emigration to New York. Many immigrants moved to Chicago because of economic and agricultural hardships. There was an advertisement below the article: "Beyond the ocean, a new chance awaited those who could save up or borrow money to get a prepaid ticket from a relative who lived in the promised land. After several crop failures, 1867 became the 'wet year' of rotting grain, 1868 became the 'dry year' of burned fields, and 1869 became 'the severe year' of epidemics and begging children."

The article ended by stating that "more than sixty thousand Swedes left their homeland during the three 'starvation years,' desiring to find a better life in America. The larger portion eventually settled in the cities."

The Long-Kept Secret

New York was the key to many job opportunities. After the Civil War, an increase of immigrants traveled to the harbor in an attempt to fulfill their ambitions. They left their homelands due to politics, economics, agriculture, or disease. Suzanna knew that her timing was impeccable. New York was a beacon of light, inviting the downhearted, challenging the aspiring, and leading the country with its great diversity of people into a new age of progress.

She focused on a small picture of John D. Rockefeller. He was one of the most successful oil tycoons in the nineteenth century. In 1863, he began the production of kerosene. By the end of the 1860s, the production of oil tripled.

A gray-haired man with a tall, black hat knocked on Suzanna's compartment door. "Pardon me, ma'am. My name is Calvin Cooper, and I would like to have a few minutes of your time to talk to you about a spectacular business venture. I'm a close friend of Mr. Irving's. He informed me of your travels to New York."

"Oh yes," she responded.

"Miss Montgomery, I've been traveling for the past few months trying to find some intelligent people who would take some time to listen to me on a business venture that I guarantee will bring in as much money as the gold rush." His eyes were piercing and fixed on her face as he sat down across from her.

"May I offer you some tea?" she asked.

"Oh no, thank you. I'll pass. I'm a coffee drinker," he responded.

Lily giggled at his remark.

"I see you've been reading about Mr. Rockefeller. Believe it or not, he is a great friend of mine. He shared his dreams about the oil refinery in the early 1860s. I should have become one of his partners. I was preoccupied with other business ventures. You've got to take a risk to make it big in any industry." He smiled and reached for some papers. "Like Irving, for example, the production of cigarettes will be in great demand one day. It just takes some time."

Suzanna nodded. His timing was impeccable, and she was intrigued. She had transferred all her money to a New York bank and was waiting for a great idea, an investment that would make her

Alexandra Lamour

money grow immensely. She looked at the papers on the food cart. There were sketches of all shapes and sizes of canned foods.

"One of Napoleon's greatest inventions," he said. "He was so busy conquering Europe that he wasn't aware of the enormous impact of canned foods."

"I see your point, Mr. Cooper. The only problem is there are a large number of people who will only eat fresh foods. During the war, I ate some canned foods and nearly fell ill. The food was bland and tasteless—yet it saved my life."

"There will be hard times again, ma'am, and many other wars, I guarantee. I am looking for some investors. I need a lump sum of money by the middle of June so that we can start building the factory. I have chosen a prime location: New York Harbor."

"How much do you need?" she asked as she poured herself more tea.

"I need an investor at 10 percent of the company's value. The amount of money for investors is going to be reviewed by my attorney."

She tried to remain professional and unexcited. She loved the idea, and Mr. Cooper didn't need to convince her anymore. Many immigrants were flocking to the city, and canned foods were the best way to feed them and preserve food for a lengthy period. It was a genuine investment. She looked up at him and smiled.

"I gather that means yes?" he asked.

"How could I refuse?" she said.

"We need to meet with my lawyer to discuss the contract."

"Of course, Miss Montgomery. Here is my card. Once you have settled in, I will give more details and pertinent information on your investment."

He bowed, put on his hat, and departed the compartment.

Once he was out of sight, Suzanna turned to Lily and said, "Mr. John D. Rockefeller, look out and make room for Miss Suzanna Montgomery. My success has just begun. I believe this is a profitable investment." It was her first investment.

The Long-Kept Secret

The train was approaching New York. Their arrival would be within the hour. It would be a new experience. She gathered her belongings, ready to defy anyone who stood in her way.

"Lily, let's try to exit the train before the rush. We mustn't dally. Goodness gracious, there are so many people."

"Yes, Miss Suzanna, I think I have everything."

On the platform, people were rushing to board the train, pushing and shoving through the crowd. With a snap of her fingers, Suzanna flaunted a silver coin in her lovely hand and beckoned a porter to assist with their baggage. Two black horses pulled their carriage to the apartment. The streets were busier than in Charleston, and people were everywhere.

"Boy, Miss Montgomery, city folk are sure a lot noisier than country folk. Everyone is in a rush."

A man drove past them in his wagon. He was hollering and whipping the horse, demanding to pick up some speed.

"Yes, they sure are, Lily. Life will be very different here." Her mind was absorbed in tallying up her funds. If she didn't invest her money wisely and continued to live an extravagant lifestyle, there would not be enough funds for the future. She forced herself to shake off such negativity. *That will never happen to me. If I have to become a miser and pinch every penny, I'll do it,* she believed. Her childhood had taught her so much about survival with little means. If she could survive her past, the future would never be a concern.

Their apartment was on Thirty-Second Street. Suzanna instructed the driver to take a left on Thirty-Fourth Street. With his thick accent, light hair, and skin tone, she presumed he was a Swede. The carriage came to a halt in front of a three-story apartment building. Its brand-new appearance was so different from the crippled buildings in the South after the war. It was charming, and she favored it at once.

A very old lady stood at the top of the stairway with some papers in her hand. Her dark cotton dress complemented her face. Mrs. Johnson, the landlady, had been widowed during the Civil War and had lost her only son a few days before the South surrendered. Suzanna reminded Lily about the importance of getting the apartment

Alexandra Lamour

as soon as possible so it would be presentable to guests. Order within a household helped keep order in her mind. She hated the thought of boxes and baggage taking up space for days.

"I see that you finally made it," Mrs. Johnson said. "Here's your key and some papers for the six-month lease."

"Yes, Mrs. Johnson." If Mrs. Johnson truly despised Southerners, Suzanna wondered if it would be better to choose another apartment.

Lily remained silent, avoiding eye contact with the landlady.

The apartment was located on the top floor. The stairs were difficult to climb after their lengthy journey. Suzanna turned the large key and flung open the door, relieved to see some pieces of furniture in the salon. She threw off her hat and took in the most spectacular view. From a distance, she could see the harbor. There were many ships at the dock; one was making a magnificent entrance, its horn attracting the attention of her audience.

Lily gasped at the spectacular size of the vessel.

Everything was moving so quickly.

"We need to purchase some food. Let me change, and I'll go with you," Suzanna said. "Hopefully, there is a market nearby."

"Yes, ma'am. I'll be ready in a few minutes.".

The market was busy with customers. When Suzanna approached the fruit and vegetable stands, she was shocked by the exorbitant prices. A dozen eggs cost a nickel, a pound of apples cost a dime, a pound and a half of butter cost eight pennies, and cheese cost six pennies a pound. Suzanna purchased a lot of fruits and vegetables, some meat, and a small packet of fish. Suzanna ate fish regularly since she knew it possessed a lot of nutritious oils.

"That will be one dollar and two pennies." The clerk wiped his dirty hands on his stained apron. His teeth were dirty, and his smell was unbearable.

Suzanna was eager to pay and get out of his presence.

"Such a fine-looking lady you are," he added.

Suzanna cringed.

"You look like one of those Southern belles, looking so fine."

The Long-Kept Secret

"Come, Lily," Suzanna said. "It is important never to challenge a man—even though this one almost put me in a frenzy. Such a fool."

Lily arranged the food in the kitchen. The milk bottle accidentally slipped from her hands and crashed onto the floor. She picked up the broken pieces of glass from the puddle of milk. "I'm so sorry, ma'am! It slipped from my hands." She began to cry.

"Lily, it's not worth crying over spilled milk," Suzanna said.

"This is more than spilled milk. What is happening?"

"I don't feel right here. There are so many new things to learn. Country folk and city folk are so different. I fear I'm not going to be able to adjust." She wiped a tear from her big brown eyes. "Miss Montgomery, I don't think I'll ever fit in." Her chest heaved up and down, and her voice squeaked.

"Hush, Lily. You would have never come all this way if you weren't sure of what you wanted—and you have the freedom to come and go as you desire. I would never force you to remain in New York if you were ever unhappy. Give it a while, and if things don't turn out how you hoped, I would willingly have you sent home. Give it time, Lily. It would help to explore the freedoms you never had in the South. Remember, the North is much more liberal and open to people's rights."

Suzanna bent down to help her. She saw a side of Lily hidden for so long on the plantation. She thought of Lily as a younger sister. Suzanna patted her back and told her everything would be all right.

111

Chapter 17

The following week, Suzanna sent for Mr. Cooper.

He appeared at the door early in the afternoon. His attorney's glasses and grim face made her feel uneasy. His voice was direct. He spoke about the significance of covering every detail. He made a quick bow of his head and removed his hat. Then they walked to the table.

The lawyer said, "It was brought to my attention the other day that Mr. Cooper has your consent to invest a substantial amount in his new project, which will not materialize for several months. These papers state that you agree with the amount of the investment to be paid in total by the date mentioned at the bottom." He squeezed the right side of his glasses, drawing them closer to his eyes.

Mr. Cooper shuffled the papers before him, pointing out several lines about the consequences of breaking the agreement. He rambled on and on, not allowing Suzanna to get a word in edgewise. He discussed the potential profits and risks of losing a substantial amount if things went sour, and he repeated certain areas of concern.

He must think I am inexperienced, Suzanna believed, *and an uneducated female. How dare he continue so long without giving me a chance to speak!* "I am unaware of the amount of funds needed for my investment." Her Southern drawl amused the attorney.

The lawyer continued to read the papers spread out before them. Finally, he said, "Mr. Cooper will discuss the amount later."

The Long-Kept Secret

"Our friendly conversation on the train only pertained to my possible agreement if the price is right and if all goes as planned." She poured some tea for the lawyer and a cup of coffee for Mr. Cooper. He focused on the papers and his attorney's face.

Mr. Cooper said, "Miss Montgomery, I would like you to visit the factory under construction at the harbor. Shall we?" He stood up and waited for Suzanna to gather her belongings.

Lily would be joining them. Leaving her apartment alone with two men was highly inappropriate. She refused to make a spectacle of herself, and she had to keep her name spotless. Nothing could damage her reputation. Becoming a social outcast was as bad as experiencing a slow death.

They all boarded a flashy carriage, and the footman bowed his head and clicked his heels. The day was beautiful, and the sun was smiling at her decision. A different kind of satisfaction soared through her being; it was the feeling of joy that she had initiated. *If only they could see me now, those boring people back home, following the same regular routines, nothing ever changing.*

New York Harbor had crowds of people busily walking in different areas of the dock. Many ships were unloading goods and supplies. One ship seemed to have recently arrived as a mass of people descended the ramp. The smaller vessels were for private enterprises, mainly in the seafood, clothing, and textile businesses. Several men were constructing the factory. Wooden sheds stored tools and equipment. The facility had large slabs of wood lying about. Workers loaded supplies on hand carts and wagons. The factory was a work in progress.

Mr. Cooper said, "Most of the employees are poor immigrants. There are a lot of Irish, Italians, British and Germans. Their eagerness to work is quite apparent by their enthusiasm."

"Yes, I can see it is quite evident."

To be employed was considered a big deal for any immigrant who had left a disheartening homeland.

Mr. Cooper was respectful toward his workers. He spoke to them in private, causing a roar of laughter. He walked back to Suzanna to

Alexandra Lamour

discuss the cost of the project and the amount of time it would take to complete. It was speculated to take twelve to eighteen months, depending on accessible materials and supplies.

"Well, Miss Montgomery, I hope you like what you have seen. I want to show you some of the sketches."

The footman gave him the drawings, and Suzanna wondered what it cost Mr. Cooper to keep two employees for one carriage. He seemed to have expensive taste.

"The factory is going to be two stories high. There will be approximately sixteen rooms, requiring anywhere from seventy-five to eighty employees. Right now, the minimum wage is a dime an hour. The monthly expenses will be nearly three hundred dollars a month. For all of us to make a decent profit, the factory needs to generate a gross income of at least three to four times the monthly expenses. So far, there are three other investors, not including yourself, ma'am."

"Mr. Cooper, if I wish to become a partner at 10 percent of the business, what will it cost me?"

"At 10 percent, it will cost you roughly two thousand dollars."

The lawyer handed Cooper more papers and remained silent.

"I need at least 50 percent to get the ball rolling. I'll need the other half before the end of next month." He looked at her and waited for a response.

She said, "Mr. Cooper, I must say, I wasn't anticipating spending that much money, especially after we spoke a few days ago."

"Don't take too long. Remember that I have other investors in mind."

After selling the plantation, she had about twenty-five thousand dollars in the bank; the other half had gone to Fuchsia's beneficiaries.

Cooper called the driver by name, and they drove off toward her apartment.

She was making a choice without a guaranteed outcome. Skepticism filled her mind as she looked out the window. She wanted a decisive answer. If she had someone to give her advice, it would make everything so much easier. Claudette would know what to do since she was a shrewd businesswoman, but Mr. Cooper seemed to

The Long-Kept Secret

be an honest man. The first step in the partnership was trusting him with her investment.

The carriage stopped in front of her apartment, and Mr. Cooper made eye contact with her. "Shall I dare ask your response—or is it still too soon?"

She took a deep breath and said, "Yes, I would love to invest in your company."

The signed contract that afternoon made Suzanna feel luckier than she had felt in a long time. Optimism filled her being as she thought about her future. "It looks very promising, and for the first time in my life, I truly believe in myself."

"I'm very happy for you, ma'am," Lily answered.

"This will be one of my biggest business accomplishments."

Her outlook on life had altered tremendously, and she could sense that prosperity was just around the corner. She had promised to donate a portion of the profits to a local charity in memory of Fuchsia since there had been so many needy organizations since the Civil War ended.

Chapter 18

Two years had passed since the closing of Suzanna's most beneficial business venture. The profits from the factory doubled after the first year and tripled in the second year. "Calvin Cooper Enterprise" had caused a couple of the smaller canned food businesses in the area to close quickly, swallowing them up like a great white shark. Mr. Cooper implemented the same strategies as the big companies that controlled the raw materials, transportation, manufacturing, and distribution. In Suzanna's eyes, he was a genius, and she looked up to him with respect and admiration. He was almost like a father figure for her.

The celebration of the factory's success was to take place at the Coopers. Mr. Cooper invited many influential people and investors to his home on Long Island. Suzanna spent an entire morning debating over her wardrobe. Finally, she chose the expensive dark red sequin gown, a ruby and diamond necklace, and a matching bracelet she had purchased in Paris. As she looked at her reflection, she thought of Edward. Painful memories still plagued her. It was impossible to shut him out of her life!

"Oh, how I wish I could attend!" Lily buttoned the tiny silver buttons on the lower part of her dress.

"Lily, I promise you, one day you will," she said with a smile.

Suzanna dreamed of living in a home where she could have many social gatherings. After all, she was on her way to becoming

The Long-Kept Secret

a prosperous woman. Her success made her very fond of New York City.

A serious discussion was circulating among the attendees that John D. Rockefeller and an English lord were coming. She couldn't recall his name. He was a cousin of Mrs. Cooper's, and Mr. Cooper wanted Suzanna to meet him.

There was a knock at the door.

Lily announced, "Miss Montgomery, Lord Waterford is here to see you."

Suzanna almost collapsed in her bedroom. She leaned against the door and said, "Did you say Lord Waterford?" *It couldn't be,* she thought.

"Yes, Miss Montgomery. He is here to escort you to Mr. Cooper's home."

Suzanna rushed to the vanity mirror and fussed with her hair and cosmetics. She had not anticipated Lord Waterford's visit. *Why did Mr. Cooper give him my address without informing me? That isn't his style, but he is such a perfect gentleman. Is this the same Lord Richard Waterford the Chevaliers told me about in Paris? The chances of meeting him were almost impossible,* she pondered. Was it coincidence or fate? She pinched her cheeks to add color. Then she straightened her gown and turned around to get a good view of its total appearance.

"Lily, could you come here. My gown has a tangle at the back, and I can't seem to reach it. Help me please."

Lily straightened the gown and puffed up the lace sleeves.

"This is remarkable. Lord Waterford is going to escort me to Mr. Cooper's party. Pinch me, please." She took one last look in the full-length mirror and turned around slowly.

"Ma'am, I must say he is very handsome and polite."

Suzanna desired to present a performance of her life after years of training under Fuchsia's wings. Her nerves got the best of her, and she fanned herself anxiously to regain her composure. She did not prepare to be escorted to the festivity by a lord. She did her best to look incredible.

117

Alexandra Lamour

She smiled, picked up her jeweled handbag, and walked to the hallway.

As she approached the lord, her pace began to slow down. She could not believe what she saw. It was as though she had been daydreaming. Their worlds joined as one entity. Her soul had been caught up in the heavens, and his presence enraptured her. He was at least six feet tall and slender; his hair was black, and his eyes were green. In his hand was his hat that matched his flattering navy tuxedo, probably the latest European design. His smile lit up the room and transcended Suzanna's heart. *This feeling is what Fuchsia described to me,* she thought.

Lord Waterford made a courtly bow.

Suzanna felt a lump in her throat and grew weak in her knees. She raised her soft hand and curtsied. "It is such a pleasure to meet you, Lord Waterford."

He kissed it and said, "The pleasure is all mine. I do hope you are enjoying the city."

"Oh, very much."

"Shall we go, Miss Montgomery?" He locked his elbow at his side, ready for her delicate arm.

"Of course. Goodbye, Lily."

"Have a wonderful evening," she replied.

He led her down the stairs, and she could not believe the carriage that awaited them. It was twice the size of Mr. Cooper's carriage. She had never seen anything like it—not even in the South, where the wealthy often flaunted their riches. It was a carriage made for royalty. A footman stood beside the opened door and motioned his hand like a maestro conducting a symphony, inviting them to enter.

Suzanna walked delicately on the step of the carriage, lifted her gown with one hand, and stretched the other toward the footman.

Lord Waterford climbed in, slightly bumping his head, and chuckled.

Suzanna laughed heartily. "Are you OK?"

"Yes, I think."

"Oh, I am glad because I left my first-aid case at the apartment."

118

The Long-Kept Secret

He chuckled. "I didn't receive an answer to my invitation requesting the honor of escorting you to the festivity."

"I highly apologize, Lord Waterford. I did not receive the message."

"Well, I must say that is indeed a relief. I thought you were avoiding me."

"Oh heavens, no," she answered and gazed at his good-looking profile.

As the horses trotted down the streets, many heads turned toward the marvelous and rare sight.

An old woman shouted, "Must be royalty!"

It took close to an hour to reach Mr. Cooper's estate. The property was on eight acres. Evergreen trees encircled the dwelling. A large iron fence surrounded the estate. The house, built in the mid-1800s, had a colonial flair. She loved the flowers and shrubbery, which could compete with any garden in the North.

Her fondness for him had grown during the journey. She remembered Fuchsia's words. True happiness in life requires opening a window to your heart. Suzanna wondered if the lord was the one she had been searching for her entire life.

He said, "I know we will have a grand time. My cousin, Charlotte, has been trying to get me to come to America for years. She thought it would do some good. Oh yes, traveling can be so rewarding. Especially when you have the opportunity to meet interesting people."

She felt a little nervous in his presence. He was a lord, and she was just a Southerner who had once lived on a tobacco plantation. *What could we have in common?* she pondered.

"And we have arrived safe and sound." He jumped out of the carriage to assist Suzanna. Her sequin gown clung to her slender body, revealing her narrow waistline. Her sparkling jewels in the sun's rays enhanced her glamorous appearance. The enchanting couple caught the eyes of many guests as they walked into the estate.

After a servant removed Suzanna's shawl, Mrs. Cooper appeared at their sides. "I hope you'll enjoy yourself, Suzanna. And, Richard, Mr. Rockefeller has not arrived yet, but I'll notify you when he does."

Alexandra Lamour

She turned to Suzanna. "Calvin has told me such wonderful things about you."

"Thank you. He has praised you on many occasions," she responded.

In the enormous salon, exquisitely dressed guests discussed the big business concept.

The wealthy and aristocratic realm was intriguing. Suzanna allowed herself to feel right at home. The men conversed about world issues. One topic she overheard was that Queen Victoria's popularity was at its peak. Despite the monarchy's cost of four hundred thousand pounds per annum, citizens remained loyal to her. Two gentlemen were discussing the benefits of investing in a department store. It would cater to all customers' needs within one store. It was a guaranteed moneymaker. She wanted to hear more, but Lord Waterford led her to a half-empty area near the unlit fireplace.

"Her Majesty, Queen Victoria, has been in seclusion for quite a while since her husband's death. However, when we last chatted, she sounded much better—and it appears that her spirits have altered for the best."

Suzanna gazed up at him and said, "To have the honor to be acquainted with Queen Victoria. I've read so many fascinating things about her."

She knew that he knew nothing about her family. She recalled some information about her father, Lord Montgomery, and her life on the plantation. Suzanna had never known him and thought it best to conceal her past. It could jeopardize her chance of ever being with Lord Montgomery. Would he accept her illegitimate birth? Her life at the orphanage would probably bring up many disturbing questions. If he were to fall in love with Suzanna, she wanted him to love her for who she was: a Southerner.

Suzanna enjoyed tasting the best French wines and hors d'oeuvres as they circulated the room. There were a variety of cheeses, trays filled with Russian caviar, and delectable sauces for shrimp and other seafood delicacies.

The Long-Kept Secret

Mr. Cooper toasted Lord Waterford, John Rockefeller, and his other close friends and business associates.

Lord Waterford was smiling at Suzanna.

The pianist bowed his head and began to play classical music. The music of her favorite composers, Mozart and Beethoven, filled the room with jubilation as the guests prepared to dance.

"Shall we dance?" Lord Waterford took Suzanna by the hand and led her to the center of the room. The guests stood back, lining up in a circle, and prepared to watch the fascinating couple. Suzanna followed his slow, repetitive movements, and she was released and retrieved by his gentle hand. She felt like she was dancing on air. They danced in perfect rhythm.

"I've never felt like this, Miss Montgomery. You are doing something to me, and I like how it feels." He let out a hearty chuckle, and she laughed as well.

"I, too, have never felt so wonderful, Lord Waterford." She knew the night would surpass any of the past evenings. She felt safe in his arms, and she didn't want him to let her go. "Let's dance all night." She looked into his eyes. She wanted him to kiss her, but she knew it was too soon—even though his eyes showed affection.

Mr. Rockefeller was engaged in an intense conversation, probably about oil. A crowd gathered about him as he spoke with frequent hand gestures.

Lord Montgomery led her to the garden terrace. When they were alone again, he kissed her hand softly, causing her heartbeat to increase rapidly. It stimulated her body as the blood rushed through it. She smiled and tried to control herself. Fuchsia's guidance had paid off, and she felt like a princess with the world at her feet. Lord Waterford was her knight in shining armor who would rescue her from past woes.

"Miss Montgomery, I care for you deeply. You might think I am rather hasty, but I cannot hold back my feelings for you any longer. I need to know how you feel. I am not asking you to say the same— no, not yet—it would be impulsive. We've just met." He touched her golden curls and placed his arm around her waist.

Alexandra Lamour

His charisma for life and love enveloped her with hope. She did not resist. She longed for his attention.

"Tonight is perfect in every way," she stated and kissed his cheek delicately.

The couple strolled into the garden as music filled the air. The abundant stars appeared more beautiful than ever, lighting up the skies with dreams and aspirations. It was an unforgettable and magical night!

Chapter 19

The next morning Suzanna woke up in good spirits. She slept in the guest bedroom on the east end of the estate. She walked out onto the terrace and welcomed the beauty of the morning as the sun projected its rays upon the bountiful earth.

Mrs. Cooper was having breakfast alone on the main terrace. She was reading a piece of paper and then put it in her pocket.

"Good morning!" Suzanna waved.

"Good morning, Suzanna. I hope you slept well. I'm so glad you decided to spend the night."

"Yes, thank you. The festivity was wonderful."

"I'm glad you enjoyed it."

Suzanna went inside to change into the new set of riding clothes from Mrs. Cooper.

The prior evening, Mrs. Cooper had insisted that Suzanna spend the night with them because the festivity ended late. Mrs. Cooper and Richard had been close as children; she was like his older sister. He was the only son of Lord Waterford I. His father was very old and partially senile. Richard's sister, Lady Merisel, took care of him. She often meddled in other people's business and was an unlikeable person.

Suzanna went down to the terrace to have a cup of coffee and some fresh fruit. Her eyes lit up with joy when Lord Waterford approached her. He was handsome in his horse-riding clothes. His

Alexandra Lamour

presence had such power over her. His manhood, strength, and charm reflected his superb education in London.

"Well, how lucky am I? To be in the presence of two such lovely women is delightful."

"Isn't he quite the charmer?" Mrs. Cooper said and went inside, leaving the dreamy-eyed couple alone.

Lord Waterford placed his riding hat on the empty chair and sat down beside Suzanna. He admired her hair shining in the sunlight and her creamy white flawless skin.

He reached for her shoulder, brought her closer, and kissed her alluring lips. Their first long kiss was remarkable. The long-awaited kiss was worth the wait and lingered in her thoughts for a while.

"I've been impatiently waiting for you all morning," he said.

"I have been restless for the morning."

He held her hand and kissed it softly. "Oh my. No woman in all of England moves me like you do."

"I could barely wait to see you, Richard." She reached for his arm, hoping he would kiss her again.

Instead, he gazed straight ahead and explained the British way of riding in a sincere voice. He sounded like a nobleman.

"Shall we go, my dear Suzanna?"

"Yes, of course, my dear Richard."

She happily thought of their life together as they walked toward the horses. A servant was holding the horses' reins, trying to soothe the brown one as they approached. Richard called out to it by name and began to pat its face in a circular motion, immediately calming the horse.

They mounted their horses and rode toward the woods behind the estate. There wasn't a soul in sight. The shrubs and trees completely blocked the view of the home. They were alone and looked forward to sharing their time in private.

"Suzanna, I plan on leaving next week for London. My father has fallen ill again." His eyes were focused directly ahead of him.

Suzanna felt a heavy pain in her heart. She bit her upper lip to prevent it from quivering. She felt so confused. Why had he brought

The Long-Kept Secret

her so far just to let her down? *Perhaps he realizes our worlds are too different,* she contemplated. *Maybe the chance of us being together is ridiculous.*

She had to tell him about her father. It was the only way she could meet him halfway. Keeping the truth from him was tearing her up inside. Her secret would be revealed eventually. It was best to tell him now. After a quick prayer of faith, she said, "Lord Waterford, my late father, Lord Montgomery, immigrated to Charleston from London for a business venture."

He jerked the horse's rein and came to a stop. "*Lord* Montgomery?" He jumped off his horse and took her hand. "Suzanna, I don't understand why you have kept this secret from me?"

Tears filled her eyes. She tried to tell him more, but the timing was all wrong. "Can we talk somewhere else? I can't explain it to you here. It's a delicate topic."

"Absolutely." His expression was solemn. "Let us return at once."

She hoped the information would not alarm him and alter everything they had planned together.

They mounted their horses and headed back to the home. She raced faster than he did, and by the time he arrived, Suzanna was standing by Mrs. Cooper.

Richard dismounted and walked toward the two women.

Suzanna began, "First, I want to apologize for my behavior." She reached out to him.

He said, "You didn't give me a chance to tell you how I feel, and I want you to listen to what I need to say."

Tears filled her eyes. His heart seemed genuine, and his words were worthy of being heard.

Lord Waterford caressed her cheek and pressed his body toward hers, making her feel safe. She freed herself from him and said, "My late father was indeed Lord Montgomery; however, my mother was never a lady." She paused to clear her mind. Revealing her past would unveil a part of her very being and free her soul. If he knew the truth, she had nothing to fear. If the truth forced them to separate it was never meant to be. She scrutinized his face, wondering if he

Alexandra Lamour

would reprimand her for such boldness. "I never knew my mother. All I know is that she was my father's British servant. They had a secret love affair, and she fled the household when she was expecting me. I was placed in an orphanage after her death and lived there for several years. My father, Lord Jonathan Montgomery, never knew of my existence. He was indeed a lord, Lord Montgomery, and my dear poor mother ... died the day after my birth."

Suzanna turned her head in another direction and waited for his response. She could hear the sound of the ocean and wanted it to engulf her to sweep her away. She wanted to run afar but instead froze in her spot. She felt unworthy to be part of Richard's life. Was her past so bad that it could ruin any chance of a future with him?

His hesitation spoke for itself. He paced around the terrace with his hands clasped on his lower back—just like Edward.

Would her illegitimate birth be a disgrace in his eyes? Was their love going to be lost because of something Suzanna had no control over? Would his social status take precedence over his love for her?

He stopped walking and turned to her.

All at once, she felt faint. How would she endure rejection? Perhaps he believed it would be best to sever what they had so far. It seemed like an eternity as she waited for his response.

His hand reached for hers, taking away the pain of her childhood. "Your past is the past. Our love is now. It is now, darling, that matters most. Not a past that you had no control over. I love you, Suzanna, and I want to make you my wife." He pulled her closer.

"Oh, Richard!" she shouted. "I love you!" His warm lips touched hers, causing a tingling feeling throughout her body. It energized her desires. She caressed his dark hair. Then she gazed into his loving eyes.

He said, "I was trying to explain my intention of returning to England and my wishes to make you my wife, but you rode off like a silly goose."

She giggled. "Oh, so I looked like a silly goose?"

Richard led her to a stone bench, and they shared their dreams. Suzanna would become a woman of nobility. It also meant relocating

The Long-Kept Secret

to another country and having a fresh start. She decided not to relinquish her investments in Cooper Enterprise in case things ever went stale. She was clever with money, and she understood how merciless life could be without it.

Lord Waterford took out a small velvet case and passed it to Suzanna. It contained the most stunning ring she had ever seen. The ruby had several pear-shaped diamonds around it. He placed the ring on her finger.

"Oh my! I've never seen anything so beautiful."

"We will celebrate tonight." He took her delicate hand. "I know it will be hard for you to give up your homeland, but I promise you that we can return here whenever you want."

Mrs. Cooper met them on the terrace and congratulated Suzanna with a kiss and a warm embrace for Richard. "At our first meeting, I knew you were the perfect match for Richard." She led them into the library and showed them one of her favorite wedding pictures.

"Oh, you both looked so charming," Suzanna said.

Mrs. Cooper reminisced for a moment and responded, "Yes, we did. And how the years have passed! We must prepare for an engagement celebration before you leave, Richard."

He consented with a quick nod and turned to his fiancée.

Suzanna squeezed Mrs. Cooper's hand.

Lunch, a feast prepared for royalty, was served promptly at noon. A variety of hor d'oeuvres were on gold-rimmed plates. There was a wide range of shellfish cooked in garlic and butter. Suzanna and Richard ate veal cooked with cheese and tomato sauce for the main course. A servant dressed in perfect attire poured chardonnay. Mrs. Cooper's final nod showed how pleased she was with the meal.

Mr. Cooper turned to Richard and said, "You have made an ideal choice. I'm so pleased for the two of you. I wish you both much happiness and success in your marriage."

"Thank you, Mr. Cooper," Suzanna said.

"We appreciate your good wishes," added Richard.

The luncheon included Italian desserts served on a silver tray. Suzanna ate chocolate cake smothered in chocolate sauce with nuts and crushed raspberries. Richard ate a cannoli topped with cream.

After the meal, Suzanna went to the guest chamber. A servant brought in her baggage and placed it beside the bed. The room was three doors down from Richard's room. She changed her clothes and walked over to the window. Richard and Mrs. Cooper were in a deep discussion as they strolled in the gardens. She decided to nap and fell into a deep sleep.

Suzanna had very little recollection of her unusual dream. Struggling to push away the dark feelings, she reached for her silver brush and combed her luscious curls until she heard Richard's voice in the hallway.

She went to the salon and sat with Mrs. Cooper and Richard. "Poor child, imagine never knowing your mother and father. You must have been distraught in your childhood."

"It was difficult, Mrs. Cooper, but I'm learning to overcome some difficult memories."

"Be patient and understanding with each other. Suzanna, you have turned out to be an exceptional lady."

"Thank you for your kind words and advice," Suzanna declared. Knowing that the Coopers supported them wholeheartedly, she reached for Richard's hand.

Chapter 20

When Suzanna awoke, she went to the servants' wing to check on Lily. Her chores were easy in comparison to back home. Their visit wouldn't last longer than a few days. Once Richard left for London, they would head back to the city. She helped Lily unpack. She noticed that she was looking out of the window with intrigue. "Who are you looking at?"

"Oh, no one," Lily answered.

Suzanna spotted a tall man with dark, shiny skin and a pleasant smile working in the garden. She believed Lily had taken a fancy to him and was too scared to tell her employer, not knowing how she would react. Suzanna kept her secret close to her heart.

Lily said, "I guess I better finish gardening before it gets too hot. Mrs. Cooper has given me a few chores today."

"A gardener's work never ends," stated Suzanna. "When you think everything looks fine and dandy, more nasty weeds appear again." She paused. "What do you do but start over again? It's the cycle of life. I've had enough gardening experience to last me a lifetime."

"I guess you are right, ma'am," Lily answered.

Suzanna joined her fiancé on the terrace. Their laughter echoed throughout the property, and Suzanna reached for his hand as they waltzed around the garden. She had never shared so much joy with

129

Alexandra Lamour

another person. He brought out the best in her, and she brought out the best in him.

He stopped and said, "And this is how you greet our gracious Queen Victoria." He bowed before Suzanna with one hand behind his back and the other one holding a teacup, which spilled on his shoe.

"Richard, you are crazy this morning."

"Oh yes indeed!" he shouted. "Crazy over you, Miss Montgomery." He rushed to her side and grabbed her waist. His body was solid and warm, and she could feel his soothing lips on her neck.

"Stop," she whispered. "I think I'm going to swoon into your arms."

"Oh, goodness gracious me, no, not here." He released her body reluctantly.

"When will you depart for London?"

They held hands and gazed into each other's eyes, allowing their emotions to take precedence. He placed his head on her shoulder, and she stroked his hair. She believed it was the first time he submitted to a woman. There was no turning back. Richard had become the essence of her being.

Even though she read an article on his past lovers, it did not bother her. She recalled his comment that the past was gone and the present moment was crucial.

Mrs. Cooper handed Lord Waterford a message and left them alone.

"I will miss you dearly," she declared.

"After I settle some important matters at home, I will return as soon as possible. Please remain patient during my absence."

"Nothing could make me more patient than knowing we will be together again soon." She forced a smile.

Lily was talking to the gardener, demonstrating a daring side for the first time. Suzanna didn't want such an inexperienced girl to wrap all her dreams and needs in the first man she fancied.

"What's the matter?" Lord Waterford asked.

"Oh, it's Lily. I need to speak to her about something."

The Long-Kept Secret

"I know how much you care about her well-being. Perhaps it would be a keen decision to bring her along if she is willing to live in England."

She was relieved that he was willing to have her go with them. She kissed his cheek and rushed over to Lily.

The gardener recited Shakespeare: "Sweet is love itself possessed, When but love's shadows are so rich in joy."

The words moved Suzanna deeply. "My goodness, you did a superb job reciting Romeo's lines ... I think, Act V, Scene 1. Am I correct?"

"Yes, ma'am. I believe you are correct." He picked up his hoe.

Suzanna sat on the stone bench and said, "Lily, I have something important to tell you. Lord Waterford is returning to England tomorrow. He will be back next month."

They walked around the pond, and Suzanna added, "Lily, our reflections are images of how we see ourselves and others. The colors within us reflect our true colors." She grasped Lily's hand. "I remember you as a young girl on the plantation. I used to help you whenever you needed assistance with your duties. Remember the day I gave you your first poetry book and helped you read with expression?"

"I still have it with me."

Suzanna was worried that Lily would forget her roots. They had a unique connection. "I would love it if you could come to England with us!"

"England? Oh no! I could never move from here." She looked down at the earth. "I'd never see my folks again. Didn't you say this was the best place to live? What about your investments?"

Suzanna replied, "I will always love America. You can visit home anytime you wish."

"It's not the same. I'm growing a liking here."

"You need some time to think it over. I know what a shock this is to you."

Lily went back to the garden.

Richard approached Suzanna and said, "What did she say?"

131

Alexandra Lamour

"She needs to think it over." She took a deep breath. "I think she is becoming accustomed to New York's lifestyle."

"I want to take you to a special place today."

He led her to the carriage.

"Where are we going?"

"Where else? The theater, my darling."

"What's playing?" She sat in the carriage and straightened her dress, hoping Lily would change her mind.

"Shakespeare, of course," he answered.

They both laughed as the driver jerked the horses' reins.

PART IV

Chapter 21

1873

News of Lord Waterford's plans to marry a commoner, a Southerner, caused a commotion among the aristocrats. The lords and ladies at the royal court had some novel gossip to spread, adding spice to their monotonous daily routines. The ladies whispered behind closed doors, waved their fans in the air, and shared gossip. The lords spoke with arrogance with raised eyebrows and noses and made critical comments about choosing an American over a refined British lady.

When Suzanna and Richard returned from horseback riding, they became aware of a negative article about the couple.

Lord Waterford I said, "My, my. Such news is sheer rubbish. 'A lord falls for a Southerner.' Are there not enough ladies in London for Lord Richard Waterford?"

Richard found the article amusing. The happy couple drank tea and listened to Richard's father read the article.

Suzanna spotted Lady Merisel entering the terrace with Lady Isabella, a close acquaintance.

Suzanna was relieved Richard was at her side.

Lady Merisel said, "Suzanna, this is my dearest friend, Lady Isabella."

"It is a pleasure to meet you," Suzanna replied.

Alexandra Lamour

"Pleased to make your acquaintance." Lady Isabella forced a smile. "Richard, remember when we were children, and our parents wanted us to marry."

"You were like a sister and nothing more." He grabbed Suzanna's hand.

Suzanna declared, "Congratulations on your engagement to Lord Phillip. Merisel shared the news with us this morning."

"Thank you, we will be married soon."

As the ladies exited the terrace, Richard whispered, "She has fangs and claws, my dear. Watch out. God spared the misery of being considered for such a woman. I was relieved when I discovered her engagement." He shook his head in repulsion. "Poor Lord Phillip."

Suzanna laughed. She was aware that Lady Isabella would be a match. The tightening of her lips and shrugging of her shoulders revealed a feeling of discomfort around Suzanna. Lady Merisel's silence made her an accomplice. Suzanna's cleverness had caught the ladies off guard, and she would do her best to stop their mischievous plan.

Her future father-in-law said, "You are indeed a clever young lady. You behaved properly. I might be old, but I know jealousy when I see it. It only causes self-infliction. And I've taken a liking to you, my future daughter-in-law."

"Thank you, Lord Waterford." Suzanna was pleased to have him on her side.

Lord Waterford I stated, "Richard, she will make you a fine wife." He coughed. "Where on earth is my medicine?"

A servant wheeled him into the house.

Chapter 22

The streets were busy as their carriage passed the Tower Of London and crossed over London Bridge. The Palace of Westminster took Suzanna's breath away. Big Ben was visible from a distance. Lord Waterford made a reservation at a restaurant located near the River Thames. It was famous for England's traditional foods. Fishing boats on the river brought in fresh fish daily. The water was dark, but the waves reflected the shimmering light of the sun. Trafalgar Square was busy with people walking along the street. Richard told the driver to halt because they wanted to take a stroll.

At the restaurant, they discussed the details of their wedding. It was to take place at St. Paul's Cathedral, located on Ludgate Hill, was the highest point in the city. The wedding was scheduled for a Saturday, two weeks away. Richard's parents were married there, giving it sentimental value.

Richard chose the most exquisite wedding gown, covered in jewels and lace, created by a famous Englishman couturier, Charles Fredrick Worth. He reached great fame throughout Europe for designing original and magnificent gowns. He dictated what customers should wear, including Queen Victoria, one of his biggest fans. The queen started a trend of white wedding dresses, breaking from the royal custom, which spread rapidly throughout Europe and America.

Suzanna ordered appetizers, the main course, and dessert. Richard was impressed by her ability to take control of a situation

Alexandra Lamour

without being overbearing. His heart was in her hands, and she was careful to protect their love.

During their meal, they were interrupted many times by Lord Waterford's friends. They passed their table, made introductions, and complimented the couple. The attention they received in public made her feel so admired. They were the most favored couple in London.

Richard said, "Next time, we will sit in a more secluded area so that we can have some quiet."

"Oh no, Richard!" She leaned forward to kiss his cheek. "I love meeting your friends." She peered around the restaurant.

"I have something to share with you," he started. "We have been cordially invited to attend a festivity in honor of Queen Victoria. It is at Osborne on the Isle of Wight. Since Prince Albert's death, she has spent most of her time there."

Suzanna's eyes widened, and she looked into her fiancé's eyes. The thrilling news had put her into a jubilant state. She looked down at her food, wondering what the queen would think of her. *What should I wear? What will I say to her?* "How wonderful! Oh, Richard, I am overjoyed to meet Her Majesty." She was too timid to ask about an appropriate wardrobe and hairstyle.

He lifted his glass of wine and gazed into her eyes. Then he reached for her hand.

A second bottle of wine filled their glasses.

"May this night never end," she whispered.

"You are timeless, so beautiful."

Most of the customers had exited, and they were left alone with another couple. A talented violinist was entertaining.

Lord Waterford led her to the small dance floor, and they danced cheek to cheek. The people around them disappeared, and they were entranced by one another. In her opinion, he was the best dancer in the world. He turned her in small circles around the dance floor like Edward.

Suzanna wondered if everything around her was just a figment of her imagination. The concept of becoming Lady Waterford was too hard to conceive until she looked at him, starry-eyed, and saw him smiling with merriment. A squeeze of her hand and a warm kiss on her cheek brought her back to reality. Yes, it was true. She was the *luckiest* woman in the world. No one was ever going to come between them. Their love was invincible!

It was a little past midnight when they reached the estate. It was dark except for a light burning in Lady Merisel's bedchamber; Suzanna assumed she was working on one of her books.

The carriage came to a halt. The footman assisted Suzanna in stepping down as she held the trail of her dress. They were led up the stairs by the housekeeper with a kerosene lamp.

Suzanna declared, "Lady Merisel feels that the limitation of women's rights is a form of slavery."

Richard's voice had zeal, "I have told her such nonsense will only stir up trouble. A woman's place is in the household ———- to bear children and take care of her husband."

Suzanna ground her teeth, trying to avoid an argument. Amazingly, she had discovered something in common with Merisel and a disagreement with her fiancé.

"You can see another reason why her marriage never lasted. Father always gets into arguments with her regarding similar topics." He stopped in front of her bedchamber and made an attempt to kiss her hand.

Suzanna pulled back her hand. "I highly respect Lady Merisel's views on women's rights. If women remain subject to the male gender, there will never be any change. Women should have the right to vote, to get a good education, and the freedom to come and go as they wish. Why should it be any different for men?"

"I did not realize you felt this way. Do not be angry. Suzanna, I apologize." He motioned for the housemaid in the hallway to leave and attempted to grab Suzanna's hands.

She slowly held out her hand. "I'm sorry, Richard, but I believe women's rights are much too limited."

Richard said, "It is a delicate conversation that I think we can discuss further at another time." He smiled. "Yes, another time in the far distance."

She giggled. She kissed him on the lips and opened the door to her bedchamber.

Suzanna knew her feisty side could stir up conversations. She was glad to be able to express her view on women but disliked disagreeing with Richard. Nothing could give her the feeling of completeness that he gave her. She dismissed their conversation completely.

Suzanna awoke refreshed. She dressed and went to Richard's bedchamber. The open drapes revealed a cloudy and dreary day. Her eyes absorbed the room, and she wondered why he had not come to her first. Then, voices on the terrace traveled up to the window.

Lady Merisel and Richard were eating breakfast and were engaged in a deep discussion. She felt reassured that all was well. She joined them on the terrace and sat beside Richard.

"We will leave around noon for the church," Lady Merisel said. "Have you chosen your attire for Lady Isabella's and Lord Phillip's wedding?"

"Oh, yes. I've chosen an extraordinary gown that Richard bought me in New York." Her radiant smile caused Richard to lose his train of thought.

Their carriage arrived at St. John's Church at one o'clock. The dark sky and fog crept over the church as the lavishly dressed guests entered. Suzanna turned to reach for her fiancé's arm as she exited the carriage, smiling and giggling with delight, her face beaming. Her violet dress was made of the finest satin and had jewels around the collar. Her hair was in a bun and secured by Richard's mother's

The Long-Kept Secret

tiara. It was an heirloom passed down for generations. It sparkled like the stars.

Richard and Suzanna had read that morning about a debate regarding an aristocrat's and commoner's approaching wedding day. Below their photograph, a lengthy article talked about the preparation of a Southerner's marriage into one of England's most prestigious families. Suzanna was aware that she had become a controversial topic.

Richard gestured to the Duke and Duchess of Radcliff as they ascended to the top of the stairs.

"Richard!" The Duchess of Radcliff motioned for the couple to join them.

Beside the duchess, one of Queen Victoria's daughters, Princess Helena, gave Suzanna a half smile as she talked with the duchess.

Suzanna had never been in the company of royalty, and she imitated the reserved behavior of the women. She refrained from laughing at the duke when his enormous nose moved his spectacles as he spoke.

The Duke of Radcliff shook Suzanna's hand and kissed it respectfully.

"My, you are stunning, my dear," he began. "A rare beauty."

"Thank you, Duke Radcliff."

After she curtsied before him, he introduced the princess. Her expression and posture did not change.

The Duchess of Radcliff was captured by Richard's charm but ignored Suzanna until her husband introduced her. After a smile and tilt of her head, the duchess returned her attention back to Lord Waterford and his good looks.

Suzanna and Richard were escorted to the second row from the front. Lady Merisel sat with her father. His health had been improving the past few days, and the color had come back to his cheeks. His eyes glowed when he saw his son with Suzanna by his side. She was delighted to see her future father-in-law in such good spirits.

The pianist began with the wedding march, and the crowd stood to watch the bride escorted by Earl George. Suzanna noticed his solemn

Alexandra Lamour

face, and Lady Isabella walked like a princess with a long, flowing trail. Countess Sophia had tears in her eyes, and Lady Merisel sighed.

Suzanna looked at her future sister-in-law, trying to understand her better. From the day of her arrival, Suzanna had felt unwelcome. The sneering comments and furtive glances had created an atmosphere of unworthiness. After their marriage, when she received the title Lady Waterford, Lady Merisel would treat her with respect.

Chapter 23

The drive to the Isle of Wight took a few hours. The carriage contained Lord Waterford II, Lady Merisel, Suzanna, Lord Phillip, and Lady Isabella, and Earl George, Countess Sophia, and Lord Waterford I followed in the Guttenbergs' carriage. The sun reached its peak and shone brightly the entire day.

In Southampton, a boat was waiting for them. The noble mansion was visible in the distance. Its tower stood more than one hundred feet tall. It stood on five thousand acres. Earl George and Countess Sophia spoke highly of the immaculate gardens and ornate statues that led to the sea and private beach.

"Visitors spoke about the queen's passion for its unique design and seclusion from the heavy duties at Buckingham Palace," Lord Phillip said as he looked out the window.

Richard nodded in agreement. "I believe it gave her peace of mind, a kind of relaxation rarely found in London. Prince Albert built it for the queen as a wedding gift."

Suzanna added, "The majority of British citizens adore Queen Victoria and her determination and perseverance, which is unsurpassed by any of the queens of Europe. Furthermore, her stamina, courage to oversee people's needs, and fascination with technology make her a monumental example of the relevance of change and progress. Such qualities contribute to her success in capturing her citizens' love and support."

Alexandra Lamour

Lady Isabella was sitting quietly and not engaging in the conversation. Suzanna wanted to show that she possessed a solid education and could converse well with either gender.

Osborne House, the queen's summer residence, soon appeared.

"Close by is Barton Manor," began Richard. "It's a guesthouse for most visitors. To the left is the Swiss Cottage, once used as a playhouse for Queen Victoria's children. Correct me if I'm mistaken about nine of them."

"How quaint. It reminds me of a fairy tale lodging." Suzanna smiled in admiration.

"Yes, charming, I must say," Richard responded.

Suzanna wondered about the royal family's lifestyle at such a residence.

"Well, we won't be staying here the entire weekend," began Lord Phillip. "Unfortunately, we must return to London tomorrow due to a business meeting."

"Yes, Father's condition could alter at any time, leaving him at the mercy of an unfamiliar physician. We will leave with you both," stated Lady Merisel.

Suzanna's room was beside Lady Isabella's, which made her a little uncomfortable. Richard's room was on the opposite side of the hallway, next to Isabella's parents. Suzanna's baggage was delivered to her chamber before she arrived. On the table was a large crystal vase of freshly cut flowers as a welcoming gift. There was enough time to reconsider her wardrobe for the ball.

Lady Isabella appeared at Suzanna's door. She had already changed into a gown. Her long black hair rested on her shoulders like Fuchsia's, which made her look even more elegant. "May I come in?"

"Of course." Suzanna was a little puzzled by her presence.

Lady Isabella sat on a cushioned chair beside a circular table.

"I must say married life can be so monotonous at times." She sneered. "Phillip is always so preoccupied with his studies in the library and periodic social gatherings at the gentlemen's club. His obsession with a scientific experiment he has been working on for a decade makes me uneasy. The other day, when I entered his

The Long-Kept Secret

laboratory, my unexpected presence almost gave him a heart attack. He nearly spilled vials of potions all over the floor. Such an odd hobby, I must say."

Lord Phillip gave Suzanna the creeps.

Suzanna believed Lady Isabella was gathering information about her relationship with Richard. She asked about the dinner celebration. "Is this your first time here?"

"No, I came many years ago with my parents. Back then, it was quite a sight for such a young lady with little experience. My parents did their best to keep me involved in all the popular social events in search of a husband. I'm sure America doesn't have balls."

"You are mistaken. There are balls amongst the very rich in the larger cities. I recently attended one with Richard at his cousin Charlotte's home."

"Oh, I see," Lady Isabella turned her head away.

Suzanna would not let Lady Isabella get under her skin. She was intuitive when it came to women's competition.

Lady Isabella rose, made an artificial smile, and lightly kissed Suzanna's cheek, "Until this evening."

"Good day." Suzanna closed the door. She knew her beauty threatened Lady Isabella. She found pleasure in watching her nervous twitches. Suzanna opened her baggage and pulled out her most stunning gold satin gown by a French couturier, Jacques Doucet. Placing it in front of her, she twirled around the room, content to know that Lady Isabella would have a fit.

Suzanna awoke from the most relaxing and refreshing sleep in a long time. She stretched her arms, arranged her disheveled hair, and glanced in the mirror. She rushed to the closet, knowing that unpunctuality was highly improper. Her biggest concern was being tardy.

Alexandra Lamour

Richard's knocking at the door made her realize she was early, causing her to rush. "Coming!" she shouted, "Give me a few more minutes, my love."

"I can't bear the wait," he said. "Must I wait another minute?" His whistling was loud enough to wake the dead.

"Oh, hush." She laughed and tried to hurry. "You must be patient, darling. You are making a fool of yourself."

"A fool for you any day," he responded.

"I'm trying to hurry," she called back. "Quiet down before Queen Victoria's guards take you away."

"All the queen's guards could not take me away from you," he said as she opened the door. "My love, you are taking me into a serene place. I believe I have just entered paradise." He reached for Suzanna's hand.

Her heart leaped with happiness.

He pulled her close, and she could feel his heart beating. She desperately wanted to remain in his arms forever. The sound of his breathing made her realize that they were one. He gazed into her eyes and pressed their bodies together.

It was time to leave. The anticipation of the grand festivity filled Suzanna with delight. She had never been to a royal ball.

The ballroom had some of England's rarest paintings and statues. A famous Italian artist designed the domed ceiling. The musicians began a minuet, one of Richard's favorites. Like a great trumpet ready to sound, the music induced the dancers to move to the center of the ballroom.

Lord Waterford swept Suzanna off her feet, and they joined the crowd. Pointing their toes, turning in circles, and greeting their partners with bows and curtsies, they danced until Suzanna had no air left in her lungs. The room twirled around her. People gathered in circles, loitered in pairs and threesomes, and whispered and chatted about the celebration. Leaving the dance floor, she waved her fan about her face.

Richard departed to get refreshments.

The Long-Kept Secret

The queen spoke with a small group at the side of the ballroom. Suzanna felt an urge to meet her to impress Richard. She kept moving backward as one person left and another filled the empty spot. The Duke and Duchess of Radcliff were standing to her right, and Princess Beatrice was to her left. She rehearsed her lines and wanted to share a few words with Her Majesty, but it was too difficult to reach her. Suzanna felt let down.

Lord Waterford returned with two glasses of champagne. He escorted Suzanna to the courtyard, and they took advantage of the ocean breezes. At the fountain, she placed her hand under the running water.

A servant brought appetizers, and they went to a secluded table. A gentleman bowed his head, and the woman waved.

Suzanna's face was gleaming in the moonlight. "Richard, this is more than I anticipated." She kissed his lips passionately. "Thank you so much for bringing me here."

They drank champagne and nibbled on Russian caviar. The servant returned with more food and drinks, but Suzanna wanted to keep her composure. They returned to the fountain, and Suzanna threw in a coin and made a wish.

Richard touched her face with his hand, moved his fingers through her hair, and declared, "I hope your wish comes true."

"It already has."

Lord Phillip bowed before them and commented, "My, my, what an enchanting place. I never realized its greatness until now." He was dressed in fine clothes, looking a little uncomfortable.

His wife, Lady Isabella, stood as straight as a peacock in a gown covered with feathers and frills.

Lord Phillip complimented Suzanna, which annoyed his wife.

Suzanna mentioned how she had seen a similar gown in a magazine. She noticed Lady Isabella's weakness. Adding more fuel to the fire, she released a pretentious smile that caused her to turn to her husband. Suzanna leaned toward Richard and whispered in his ear.

Alexandra Lamour

Lady Isabella turned to Suzanna and said, "Queen Victoria has invited us for breakfast in the morning. Did you get an opportunity to speak with her yet, Suzanna?"

"Not yet," she responded, showing little interest.

Richard said, "I think we should return to the ball. There are people I would like you to meet, my dear."

"Oh, I'd love to."

They waltzed back to the ballroom, leaving Lady Isabella with her dull husband—who wouldn't dance if his life depended on it.

The couple joined a few friends in the ballroom, adoring the music and socializing. One of Richard's closest friends appeared by his side. It was Lord Clarence Huntington III, a confirmed bachelor for life. He was a tall, overweight man with blue eyes and wavy brown hair neatly combed to the sides.

Lord Clarence said, "Richard, I knew how delighted you would be to see me again."

"Clarence!" Richard reached out his hand. "It has been a long time since we saw each other. It was last year at the London Fox Hunt Club. You were leaving for Spain to spend some time on your artwork."

"Oh, yes. I must say, you have quite a memory. I just recently returned. And congratulations on your engagement. I always believed you were a confirmed bachelor."

Richard said, "This is Miss Montgomery, my fiancée."

Suzanna lifted her hand gracefully for a handshake. Lady Merisel warned her about Lord Clarence's reputation. He was known for falling in and out of love. Crossing boundaries was also typical for him. Suzanna could feel that his eyes were set on her when Richard turned to speak to another acquaintance.

One of Richard's favorite songs began, and he reached for Suzanna's hand at once. "We shall talk again, old friend."

Lord Clarence and Richard had attended Oxford together. Even though they majored in different areas, they shared similar tastes in women and hobbies. She raised her head as they waltzed about the

The Long-Kept Secret

ballroom. She noticed Clarence's eyes following her every move, smiling with delight. He was mesmerized by her beauty.

Richard escorted Suzanna off the dance floor to replenish their thirst and left his fiancée alone. She waved her fan to calm down when she noticed Lord Clarence approaching. His direct glances at her were bold and yet appealing. Suzanna was engaged to a tremendous man. Giving her such attention was ridiculous.

Lord Clarence moved toward her and said, "No words can express the impact you have made. You are like the sunshine, illuminating my soul with its rays, yet so unique. Please do not find me offensive. I must have a few words with you."

"Oh my, another poet." She giggled. "Such words are highly inappropriate, Lord Clarence. I was recently warned about you by Lady Merisel."

His presence nearly caused her to flee in search of Richard, but her feet would not move. She was bound to the floor. *What does this mysterious man want?*

"You took my breath away on the dance floor." He bowed his head and reached for her hand.

She held tight to her fan. "Sir, I am betrothed to one of your best friends. What do you wish of me?"

"Oh my, you are a Southerner." He raised his eyebrows. "A Southern belle that captured the heart of Richard. May I ask where he found such beauty?"

When her eyes spotted her fiancé returning, she called his name. Lord Clarence bowed his head and left hastily. He was cunning and not to be trusted, she believed.

During a brief conversation, someone secretly dropped a folded paper into Suzanna's Chatelaine purse. Richard and Suzanna were too busy to have noticed while discussing politics with his old friend from Italy.

Signore Portabella was a talkative and uncouth man with a mortifying demeanor. Chewing with his mouth half opened and excessive drinking made him unappealing to women.

149

Alexandra Lamour

Suzanna went to the lavatory to freshen up. As she took out her silver brush, the folded paper fell to the floor. Deeply puzzled, she picked it up. The words were moving and tender. She lifted her hand to her chest and continued to fan her face. *Who could have written this note?* Her eyes widened. The handwriting was unrecognizable: "It doesn't matter if the sun doesn't shine or if the skies aren't blue, for my love began with you. I know this love is forever. I know that it's a must. So be gentle with my love, for it is you whom I trust."

Perhaps Richard had someone write it in jest. *How sweet.* She slipped it back into her handbag, straightened her posture, and headed for the ballroom. She would pretend she hadn't read it, making Richard wait for her response.

When Suzanna and Richard left the ball, many guests had already returned to their rooms. A foxhunt had been scheduled for the following day, organized by one of Queen Victoria's sons, Prince Arthur, Duke of Connaught. Suzanna hoped she would finally meet Her Majesty in a more relaxed setting and be able to show off her unparalleled horseback riding skills. Her mind drifted off, imagining what it would be like to live the life of a queen, a life of magnificence, and many duties to oversee.

Suzanna awoke to the sound of footsteps and paper sliding under the door. She slipped out of bed and bent down to pick it up. Thinking it was from Richard, her glowing face changed to uncertainty. She opened the door and searched the hallway, but no one was in sight. Stumbling back to bed, she lit a candle and read it. The handwriting matched the former message, and there was no signature.

"Now night had come, And all were fast asleep, And soon she heard her true love's voice, Calling from below, Awake, awake, my sweet dove, Tis I, your one true love. My masked face is for your curiosity."

The Long-Kept Secret

Preposterous! she pondered. She walked over to the window and looked down below. "Who is there?"

There was a masked man.

"Richard?" She laughed. "I know it is you."

A knock at the door mystified her, and Richard appeared like a young man in love. "You need to get some sleep." He kissed her lips forcefully. "Tomorrow will be here soon." Then he kissed her neck. His strong arms pulled her body firmly against his physique, electrifying her senses. He stroked her back and whispered, "I love you with all my heart."

"And I love you," she responded, wishing he could spend the night with her.

Concealing the recent message in her nightgown's pocket, she walked him to the door. It was best to keep the incident a secret. Whoever it was? Since she didn't feel threatened by the mysterious wooer, it was unnecessary to alarm Richard.

Her mind took another course, and she felt bold. *If this mystery man persists, I'll have to catch him myself. And whatever he has on his mind, I'll give him a lesson or two.*

She yawned and thought of all the men who had complimented her at the ball. There was Lord Phillip. Oh, heavens no! Duke Radcliff had smiled at her as she danced. And there was Lord Clarence. Possibly, it was him since he was the only bachelor at the ball. Her mind grew tired of thinking so much, and she fell asleep with both notes in the dresser drawer.

Chapter 24

The following day was ideal for a foxhunt. Richard and Suzanna had a light breakfast and headed to the central courtyard. The participants had refreshments and discussed strategies.

Duke Radcliff had the largest cluster of people around him as he spoke about the history of the foxhunt.

Suzanna caught something about it originating in the eleventh century as a method of controlling the fox population, which endangered poultry farmers. Jack Russell terriers were chosen since they possessed great speed, agility, and strength, surpassing any other kind of dog for the sport.

Lord Clarence shouted, "Richard, my dearest friend! It brings me such joy to see you again!"

Richard grabbed his friend and patted him on the back. "Clarence, it is so good to see you again! What a surprise, old chap! I believe you have already met my fiancée, Miss Suzanna Montgomery."

"Yes, of course," he said with a grin.

Suzanna smiled and turned to Richard, wondering if he had written the love notes. Toying with her whip, she spotted Queen Victoria surrounded by several people again. It was impossible to get close to her. She desired a moment with her.

The queen laughed heartily and waved her hand regally. "Let the game begin!"

The Long-Kept Secret

Cheers and shouts filled the courtyard. The crowd moved to the rear part of the grounds, rushing to get the first pick of the finest thoroughbreds in the country. The horses stood in flawless symmetry, waiting for the riders to mount.

Suzanna's expertise was evident as she jumped on the horse's back.

Lady Isabella was struggling to mount a horse while bickering with Lord Phillip.

Amused by their behavior, Suzanna turned to Richard and smiled. Shortly, he waved, signifying that they were ready to begin.

The Duke of Radcliff blew the horn to release the fox, and the ferocious hounds followed. The riders galloped with velocity after the dogs.

With whip and spur, Suzanna was leading the hunt, and Lord Clarence was right behind her. She knew she was more than a match for any rider. Her caliber and stamina showed the group that she was no ordinary woman.

The fox raced between trees, shrubs, and rocks. It went up and down slopes, visible and invisible for a few seconds, running for its life. The hounds—crazed with anger—barked and snapped at its heels.

Another experienced rider was picking up speed, leaning forward, and laughing—almost mocking her—and thoroughly enjoying the challenge of a woman. They left Richard and Clarence far behind. The excitement of the event made her forget herself. Her sweaty hands under her gloves made her push harder. The brisk air rejuvenated her body. She felt like she was home on the plantation, racing beside Fuchsia; her spirit was with her. Fuchsia was telling her to pick up more speed. She felt as free as a bird, carefree and proud that she would be praised and recognized by Her Majesty. It would be the most outstanding achievement of her life!

The expert rider began to lose his speed, and Suzanna leaped over some fallen trees. She continued to keep him at a far distance. She knew that he would be appalled for being outrun by a female would be one of the biggest humiliations of any male's life.

153

Alexandra Lamour

The feeling of victory was within reach. She laughed at the uproar that she would cause among the British citizens. What a Southerner! The only thing on her mind was staying as close as possible to the hounds and keeping her focus.

The fox ran into a burrow, and the dogs finally caught up to the creature—more furious than ever. The ferocious yelping and squealing signified the hounds had trapped the fox.

Suzanna yanked on the horse's reins, trying to tame it. She looked behind her and noticed her rival approaching. The unfamiliar face was smiling and laughing—but too breathless to speak. She tried to slow down her breathing by exhaling slowly. The results of the hunt would make her the talk among the guests.

Richard and Clarence arrived, and both men were breathing heavily. They were speechless and astounded.

Finally, Richard said, "My dearest, you are simply divine. I have never—in all of my years of riding—witnessed such a phenomenon."

"Nor have I." Clarence wiped his forehead with a handkerchief.

"Please, Richard, have them trap and spare the fox's life. I would hate to feel partially responsible for its death."

"Of course, spare the fox's life!" he shouted.

A servant with a cage trapped it.

Richard said, "It's not customary, but for you, anything."

Sir Gregory Arlington, who the queen had knighted before Prince Albert's death for his outstanding medical contributions to England, was one of the queen's most trusted physicians. He dismounted his horse, mortified by his first loss in over a decade. Queen Victoria and the Duke of Radcliff would present the trophy to the superior rider of the event. Curious eyes surveyed the group and waited for the gentleman to step forward.

A contestant shouted, "Again, Sir Gregory—for the tenth time in a row—has won!"

Another spectator yelled, "No, it was a woman. I witnessed her arriving first!"

Suzanna clenched her whip tightly. She believed she would not be recognized to prevent disgrace amongst the males.

The Long-Kept Secret

Richard and Clarence were absorbing the queen's speech.

Suzanna watched admiringly as the queen thanked her family and guests for their support and unconditional love. She declared, "One rider showed good sportsmanship, excellent skillfulness, and foremost, set a record for the swiftest rider today. It gives me great pleasure to introduce Miss Suzanna Montgomery, Lord Richard Waterford's fiancee." She raised the trophy in her regal hands. The queen's smile lit up the skies.

Suzanna's heart fluttered. She had done the impossible! It was the highlight of her life!

Richard whispered, "You are a sight to behold."

"Richard, I will remember this moment forever. The Queen of Great Britain will give me a trophy!" Suzanna saw some arrogant looks and heard the whispers of a man wondering how a young lady could have beaten Sir Gregory.

Richard whispered, "You are causing an upheaval in the crowd. Be careful."

"I don't care." She laughed. "And let the envious be consumed by jealousy." She knew the men felt it was disgraceful to place the trophy into a woman's hands. She overheard a couple of males say it was comical to see a woman receive honor from Her Majesty.

Suzanna squeezed Richard's hand as he escorted her toward the platform. The crowd parted and gazed upon this enchanting and well-proportioned goddess. Suzanna saw Lady Isabella frowning at her.

The queen waved her elegant hand and said, "It has always been my firm belief that women's functions in life are more than bearing children. We are a beacon of light setting forth the pathways for our husbands and children, inspiring the world. We will not have failure, only success. She turned to Suzanna. "Always believe in yourself, and you shall move mountains." She whispered, "Behind every success is a woman, and I, for one, am living proof of this."

"Thank you, kindly, your Royal Highness. I will always remember your words." Light filled her eyes, and she curtsied and kissed the queen's hand. Suzanna handed the trophy to Richard as

Alexandra Lamour

they descended the stairs. "I will cherish this trophy for the rest of my life. I can't believe Queen Victoria gave it to me."

Richard said, "It was sufficient that you were every woman's envy and every man's fantasy at the ball, but now to receive the fame and acknowledgment of the queen is too much for their stirred-up hearts to contain."

The crowd roared with excitement as they stood in front of the platform. All eyes were on Suzanna and Richard. As they passed through the people clapping and shouting, a past memory flashed before her. Everything she had experienced was for a reason, and the events of her life had brought her to this place and time.

As the cheering slowly subsided, there was a minute of silence. The crowd stopped to face the queen again.

Everyone sang with their hands placed over their hearts during a patriotic song. The military officers saluted the queen. When the song ended, the people cheered again. Many people surrounded Suzanna and congratulated her as they walked to the main hall for the feast.

The Duke of Radcliff kissed Suzanna's hand and said, "Richard, I would always keep her in your sight. She is no ordinary woman."

Richard smiled and said, "I must say … I *do* agree."

Chapter 25

At the crack of dawn, Suzanna gathered her belongings and packed them. She remembered the importance of meeting Richard on the terrace at sunrise. She dressed quickly and double-checked the room. The letter she had written to the queen showed her gratification for a time well spent, a time filled with enduring recollections. She sealed the envelope and left for Richard's room.

In the hallway, she gave the letter to a servant and asked him to deliver it to the queen. The door sprung open as she was about to knock. Richard held flowers in his hands. They shared breakfast on the terrace, watching the sunrise in each other's arms.

"We will have an eternity of sunrises together," he said. "It's amazing!"

"What is?"

"How the simple everyday routines appear so much more beautiful and exciting when you are in love."

"Oh, yes. I know what you mean. Richard—and you'll love me forever and ever, never allowing anyone or anything to ever come between us?"

"Nothing—and no one!"

They were ready to go home, but they were disappointed that the excitement had ended so rapidly. There were so many things to attend to. The wedding was first on the list. By the middle of the day, they were on the outskirts of London. While leaving a world of peaceful

Alexandra Lamour

nature and entering one of liveliness, their duties became a priority. The ornate carriage approached the charming city, riding on the horizon like a scene from a magazine.

At last, the journey ended. As the carriage turned down the road to their dwelling, the iron gates appeared to be questioning their whereabouts. The branches of the trees hovered, bowed, and beat against the walls as they drew nearer. When the carriage door swung open, Lady Merisel and Lord Waterford I were on the veranda.

"Did you enjoy the trip?" Lord Waterford I let out a cough.

"It was splendid, Father," said Richard.

"Yes, it was enjoyable." Suzanna tried to conceal her weariness from the journey. She wanted every family member to appreciate her for who she was.

"You are so lucky, Richard," Lady Merisel said. "It rained terribly during our return, close to two hours."

"She was as pale as death." Lord Waterford I chuckled.

"Don't mock me, Father. You know how much I detest thunder and lightning."

Lady Merisel's mind appeared preoccupied with something important throughout the dinner.

Suzanna attempted to start a conversation, but her future sister-in-law's short responses made it impossible.

When dessert arrived, Richard said, "Oh, how delicious! It's one of my favorites: crème caramel."

"I asked Pierre to make it, especially for you!"

The couturier interrupted the meal, asking Suzanna to try on the wedding gown, which was close to completion.

"I think I'll pass on the dessert. It will be easier to get into my wedding gown." She giggled.

Richard grabbed her hand as she passed him and kissed it. Her love for Richard grew every day. His every move had meaning; a touch, a kiss, and words of admiration were all part of the mystical feeling of true love.

"Don't take too long, my dearest."

She bent down and kissed his forehead. "I'm missing you already."

158

The Long-Kept Secret

The couturier had a strong French accent Suzanna had ever heard. She often switched the conversation back to his native language. He rushed about her like a madman trying to make everything perfect.

"And now, Mademoiselle Montgomery, please kindly step onto the stole. I need to examine the length." He was panting like an animal.

"You mean stool." She giggled. Then she moved at once, fearing that he would collapse from exhaustion.

He clapped his hands at his assistant to make haste with the pins. While wiping his perspiring forehead and breathing uncontrollably, his beady eyes swelled. He was the shortest man Suzanna had ever seen. His face was humorous looking. His long mustache curled at the ends. "Do I have to do everything myself? You imbecile!" He looked at Suzanna. "Excuse me, Mademoiselle Montgomery. Please take my hand. We will practice walking together in the gown. This part is most vital. And now, oui, oui, oui. Very good. Kindly turn a little to the left and now to the right. Please lift your head." He stopped to take a deep breath. "The trail, the trail, you fool!" He shouted at his assistant.

The assistant sneered behind him.

"Magnificent! A piece of art!" His face was still a little tense. "May I ask you, who will have the honor to escort you down the aisle?"

Suzanna responded, "My father passed away during the Civil War, and Richard's father is too ill. I will walk alone."

"Impossible! You must have an escort in this gown! How could you walk alone? Never! Unspeakable! I've never heard of such a thing!" He banged his foot on the floor.

As they walked around the room, the assistant held the trail to prevent it from getting caught.

"And moving ever so gently, with your head lifted slightly upward, turn with me to the right and now to the left. Yes, continue. You are a vision of beauty. You are an angel from heaven. Come this way and smile. Never stop smiling. Your wedding should be the happiest day of your life." He spoke like a ballet instructor. "You must have serious

Alexandra Lamour

eyes. Wonderful. Now stop. Please remember to stop walking with a smile. Merci, mademoiselle.``

The couturier's behavior entertained her. He was also a perfectionist.

Richard had overheard the conversation. The couturier was right. It was not proper to have her unescorted. The only person who came to mind was Clarence, and they decided to contact him. Clarence would arrive at their home the following afternoon. When Richard saw him in the hallway, he gestured for him to enter the library.

Suzanna sat on a sofa and listened as the two men caught up on the latest news. Finally, Richard informed his friend that they needed to discuss a personal request that touched Suzanna tremendously. She had known his love for her was sincere when they arrived in London.

While playing chess and drinking gin, Richard said, "We need to talk. Since Suzanna's estranged father died years ago, she is without an escort."

Clarence was contemplating his next move.

Suzanna did not know Clarence well enough to guess the outcome of the request. She believed Clarence was dallying intentionally.

"Yes, I see your concern." Clarence gazed around the room, avoiding eye contact with Suzanna.

Richard said, "Clarence, I must ask you for your help. The wedding is in less than two weeks, and it is troublesome to find someone worthy of escorting Suzanna down the aisle."

Suzanna was a little embarrassed by her fiancé's request. Maybe he did not want to fulfill his friend's request since they had recently met. And yet, it was a great idea to have a trustworthy friend to help in a time of need.

Clarence said, "I don't think you've ever let me down, old chap. It would bring me great pleasure to give the bride away." He reached for his cigar.

"I knew I could depend on you. I can't tell you how much this means to me." Richard slapped Clarence on the back and demanded a rematch. Then he lit up a cigar as well.

160

The Long-Kept Secret

Suzanna said, "Can you meet us at the cathedral at noon on Saturday?"

"Jolly good, my friends, and not a minute late." Clarence finished his gin and gazed at his gold pocket watch. "Sorry, I am late for a meeting. Until then!"

Lord Waterford I entered the room and said, "I've heard from the Gentlemen's Club that Clarence is in love again."

Richard laughed. "Clarence in love? That is the most outrageous thing I've heard all day. I know him too well to be unaware of this news."

Suzanna said, "Maybe he doesn't wish to share it yet."

"Perhaps? However, there is no way he could ever be unselfish and willing enough to submit to another person's needs. It's unthinkable!"

Suzanna noticed Clarence in the hallway as he straightened his hat before the gold-framed mirror.

161

Chapter 26

Buckingham Palace was one of the most iconic and recognizable landmarks in the world and was known for its superb regal ambiance. Queen Victoria's invitation to Buckingham Palace for an afternoon garden tea party had arrived at the Waterford estate one day earlier.

Suzanna appeared in Richard's bedchamber, dressed in a comfortable day dress, and she laughed when she saw him still in bed. His hair was still messy.

"Good morning, sleepyhead," she said. "I thought it over, and I think my letter to the queen made the invitation to the garden tea party possible."

"Darling, my father is good friends with Lord Chamberlain, and he creates the guest list." He kissed her chin and lips. "I haven't slept so soundly in weeks." Richard yawned and put on his robe.

"I could have stayed in bed all day." She giggled. "My bed is sumptuous and so comfortable. By the way, I hope I can find something appropriate to wear for tomorrow."

"Mary will help you," he said. "She has a talent for these kinds of things."

"I am delighted about tomorrow. I have only seen the palace at a distance."

"We passed it during our first carriage ride. Did you know it has been in the hands of the British monarchy for more than four hundred years?"

162

The Long-Kept Secret

"Yes, I read a book in the library about the palace's history. It rests on thirty-nine acres and has at least seven hundred rooms, including bedchambers, lavatories, ballrooms, and staff rooms."

"My, you have done some research already." He smiled. "Don't forget the staterooms ... since it is the British monarchy's administrative headquarters."

Coffee and crumpets were served on the table by the window. Suzanna was glad to see her favorite raspberry preserves on the plate with different kinds of cheeses. Her appetite increased after the first bite of the crumpet, and she ended up eating more than usual. "I better be careful—or my waistline will be horrendous."

"Don't worry. It has been dismal this week, but the sun is finally shining. After breakfast, we will go for a long walk."

After breakfast, Mary helped Suzanna choose her garden party attire. They chose a white dress with lace around the neckline and cuffs. Her hat, made from the same material, had pink roses on one side. It matched the dress and her parasol. A pearl necklace and bracelet from Charleston completed the ensemble. Mary also helped Richard choose one of her favorite black three-piece suits and a black top hat.

Lady Merisel declined the invitation since she had a sore throat.

The next afternoon, Richard, Suzanna, and Lord Waterford I boarded the carriage for Buckingham Palace. The garden party would take place on the five-acre chamomile lawn between the front garden of the palace and the lake. There were numerous tea tents as a protection from sunlight. Suzanna thought it was sweet how her future father-in-law walked with the help of a cane. He refused the wheelchair, which would have been a nuisance with the crowds.

The rows of carriages stationed in front of the palace arrived before their arrival. Lord Chamberlain personally greeted them. He was a very tall man with a crooked back. "Bartholomew!" Lord

Alexandra Lamour

Chamberlain shook Lord Waterford's hand and then Richard's. He bowed to Suzanna like a perfect gentleman.

"How have you been?" asked Lord Waterford I.

"I am wonderful and grateful for so many family blessings," he responded.

As Lord Chamberlain led them through the palace, Suzanna's eyes absorbed the most extravagant paintings, decorative ceilings, fireplaces, and gas-powered lighting she had ever seen. She noticed the polished floors and Wilton carpets. There was a large painting of the queen and the prince with their children around them. "Everything looks extraordinary, intricately designed for royalty," she whispered to Richard.

"Indeed," he answered. "I haven't been here in years. Many things have changed."

Before they reached the gardens, Lord Chamberlain turned to discuss Queen Victoria's assassination attempt the previous year and how pleased he was that it had failed. "The madman entered the fence over there and crossed the courtyard without detection. Her Majesty had just returned to the palace entrance when he raised a pistol just a foot from her."

"Yes, I believe his name was Arthur O'Connor," Lord Waterford I said.

Lord Chamberlain said, "He was a descendant of Irish revolutionaries. We believe he wasn't going to kill her. He wanted to frighten her into releasing Irish prisoners from British jails." He led them to a table close to the queen.

Long tables held salmon and cucumber and shrimp or anchovy sandwiches, tea scones, mango and strawberry custard tartlets, and cakes. Servants catered to all the guests.

Every table had a large teapot and several English bone china teacups. Queen Victoria's specially prepared sponge cake with strawberry preserves in the middle was sliced and placed on porcelain plates with patterns of flowers and nature scenes.

The white tents sat on well-maintained grounds of the palace with brilliant flower beds, shady arbors, and splashing fountains adding charm to the event.

The Long-Kept Secret

The Waterfords' tent was close to a fountain. There were friends of Lord Waterford I sitting close by. Suzanna's beauty captured the attention of many guests.

"Lord Richard, would you like some tea?" Suzanna asked.

"Of course. I must say we have the prettiest hostess at the festivity." He lifted his cup.

"Lord Waterford, may I?"

He waved his hand in refusal.

Queen Victoria stood up and said, "It gives me great honor to first thank our war veterans who have served Great Britain over many years. I salute all of you for your outstanding hard work and love for your homeland."

The people cheered and clapped as the veterans stood up at their tables, bowing their heads and waving to the people. One particular war veteran gave a speech that moved Her Majesty.

"Furthermore, Prince Albert and I have always been grateful to our loyal staff members and British citizens for their ongoing commitment to Great Britain. Please enjoy the food and, of course, my favorite sponge cake." She waved and resumed her seat.

Lord Waterford I conversed constantly with some old friends from Parliament and then ate his cake like he hadn't eaten in days. "Scrumptious, absolutely scrumptious."

Lady Isabella and Lord Phillip were bickering as usual. When she spotted the Waterfords, she tried to appease the quarrel.

Suzanna laughed. "Richard, look over there."

"Yes, I see her hat a kilometer away. Have they not taken a break yet?" He sneered.

"I must say, they are a poor match."

"Indeed," he agreed. "I fear their marriage will not last much longer."

"This is such a remarkable event. I'm so glad we were invited." Suzanna gazed into his eyes.

"My dear Suzanna, every day we share is treasured. He drew her close and held her tight. No one else could make her feel so special.

Chapter 27

It was the most anticipated day for Suzzana, the wedding day. It was scheduled approximately six months after their engagement. An hour before noon, Suzanna stood in front of a full-length mirror in her white silk wedding gown; white symbolized purity, innocence, and eternal love. Cultured pearls, abundant lace, and exotic jewels were along the gown's neckline, waistline, and cuffs. A sheer veil was attached to a tiara of orange blossoms, symbolizing love's abundant joy. Feeling blessed, she wondered about married life before her for several minutes and was overjoyed.

Richard was preparing for the wedding in his bedchamber. They would be married soon and would be able to consummate their love. Richard wanted their first night together to be extraordinary.

Suzanna's wedding ring was in a velvet case in his velvet-lined jacket pocket. It had pearls and six diamonds looped in a crown setting. Richard's ring was crafted from gold and shaped into a Roman leaf design. Lord Clarence would present the rings before exchanging the wedding vows.

A servant fixed his silk tie and made sure it rested in perfect alignment under his gray vest. His black waistcoat was short in the front and extended to the knees in the back. He wore black pinstriped pants and a black top hat.

Benet, his man-in-waiting servant, "Lord Waterford, your handkerchief."

The Long-Kept Secret

"Of course," Richard said with a chuckle.

Benet folded the handkerchief and placed it in Richard's top left pocket. "Lord Waterford, the bride is ready for the ceremony."

"Thank you, Benet." Richard took one last glance in the mirror.

Suzanna had recently read in the *Victorian Brides Magazine* that there were some superstitions about Victorian weddings. The bride had to choose the date of the wedding. June was the most popular month for marriages in England in honor of Juno, the Roman goddess of marriage. It was believed, through years of family tradition, that the goddess brought joy and prosperity to couples who married in June. The month of June also gave the bride a chance to deliver in the spring, which was a time of rebirth and renewal.

Suzanna gazed at her husband-to-be as he waited at the bottom of the stairs. Her walk was graceful as she approached him.

"Suzanna, I am madly in love with you!"

"And I love you dearly, Richard!"

Benet said, "Lord Waterford, I have known you almost all your life, and I wish you both all the happiness in the world. Suzanna is a fine lady. Remember to always be patient with each other—and never forget when and why you fell in love." He bowed his head.

The joyous couple thanked him for his sincere words. Richard shook Benet's hand and placed his arm over his shoulder. Benet was as close to him as his father, and he revered him dearly.

The two carriages containing family members and close friends accompanied them to St. Paul's Cathedral. The air was crisp and refreshing, and the sky was blue. The wedding day was perfect as she held Richard's hand. A commitment to a wonderful man was all she desired. Suzanna's wish had come true. It was an image far beyond her wildest dreams!

The carriage approached its destination, and the sound of the horses prancing became audible. Near the cathedral's entrance, a group of curious pedestrians tried to catch a glimpse of the dashing groom and striking bride in their fashionable carriage. Church bells rang when the bride arrived to ward off any evil forces.

Alexandra Lamour

The driver pulled on the horses' reins, and the footman placed a step stool before her feet.

Suzanna exited the carriage and stepped on it delicately. She was taking a big step in her life. Destiny took control of her. She was excited about the new life they would share. After they exited the carriage, Clarence reached out to shake Richard's hand.

Lord Waterford I looked distinguished with his tall black hat and suit. He was carrying a cane in his left hand since he preferred an awkward walk to a wheelchair.

Richard entered the cathedral and waited for his bride at the altar as she did the traditional wedding march.

Lady Merisel served as maid of honor, which Lord Waterford I had requested. She lifted Suzanna's train, and they climbed the stairs to the cathedral. Suzanna saw Clarence, and her white glove reached for his arm as the pianist began the music.

Lady Merisel walked down the aisle, tossing lily petals and feeling proud to be part of such an elaborate ceremony. It was far beyond her expectations. Suzanna, feeling a little nervous, took a deep breath, focused on Richard at the altar, and smiled. With a slight tilt of her head, she let Clarence know it was time to proceed. She rested her hand on his wrist, which he held as stiff as a board.

Clarence said, "My dear, as you walk beside me, I can hear the beating of your heart. I can almost feel the warmth of your breath. Grant me, fair one, a little dignity—one fair kiss upon thy cheek—so that I may remember this moment for eternity."

Suzanna continued to smile, but she was astonished by his words of passion. She whispered, "I felt that maybe it was you, but I had no proof. Your sentiments touch me. Be kind and wish us luck."

The march continued as the crowd gazed at the bride. Many were smiling, and some were mesmerized by the wedding arrangement.

Suzanna glanced to her right and spotted the Duke and Duchess of Radcliff. They were smiling as she passed them. Seeing Richard, a surge of faith and love enveloped her soul. At the end of the aisle, he reached for her hand.

The Long-Kept Secret

Clarence kissed her cheek before he released her to Richard. Then he moved to his opposite side.

Suzanna had speculated that Clarence was madly in love with her all along. It was such folly! She knew Richard would go mad if anyone or anything separated them.

The music continued, and they exchanged their vows. Richard held her hand, and her life flashed before her: her youth, life at the plantation, the Coopers, and her first encounter with Richard. Life was beautiful, and the worries and pain of the past no longer existed. What mattered was the present and relief that the wedding went as intended. Then she waited for her groom's magical kiss. Their eyes met, and she tilted her head back as his lips touched hers.

The guests clapped as the newly married couple walked arm-in-arm down the aisle.

A photographer took a picture of them in the church. Then he took another photograph of the family on the lawn. They mounted the carriage and drove off while the bells resounded throughout the streets, celebrating an unprecedented union.

"I'll love you forever," he whispered and held her close.

"Until the end of time," she responded with a sigh.

The marriage was honored by the grand feast at the Waterford Estate. A uniformed doorman greeted the guests. There were also ten servants, six chefs, and two butlers. The nagging housekeeper found fault with everything brought to her attention. Despite her disposition, meals were tasty and always served on time. Skilled cooks prepared for the guests. In the center of the garden, white tents contained numerous long tables. Each table had a fresh bouquet, well-polished silverware, gold-rimmed bone china plates, and Czechoslovakian crystal glasses waiting for the finest wines from France and Italy. Five violinists played Strauss, Beethoven, and Bach.

After the bride and groom completed their first dance, the guests filled the dance floor, twirling and stepping to the music. The musicians played slow songs and brisk melodies.

After several hours, when the celebration began to grow dim, an enormous rocket shot up into the sky, bidding the newlyweds farewell

Alexandra Lamour

as they prepared for their honeymoon. For the first time in history, it was customary for the bride to throw her bouquet from a staircase, which had become a recent tradition.

Suzanna turned around and tossed the bouquet into a young maiden's hands. "I wish you much luck, my dear!"

"Thank you, Lady Waterford!"

The sound of her new name was like music to her ears. She had never been so proud.

The extravagant carriage took them to Southampton, and they embarked on a Mediterranean excursion that was to travel to France, Portugal, and end in Sardinia. Their cliffside hotel in Italy overlooked the Tyrrhenian Sea.

Chapter 28

The *Canberra,* a notorious ship, was equipped with upper-deck compartments, restaurants, shops, a library, and a billiard room. More than six hundred people boarded the enormous ship.

Their suite had a superb view of the ocean. Suzanna undressed in the adjoining lavatory and put on a sheer white nightgown. She knew Richard was also changing in the room. When she stood at the doorway, Richard was speechless.

Finally, he approached her and said, "I have never seen a more beautiful sight."

"You are the best-looking man I have ever met."

She touched his face as he moved closer. He pressed a warm kiss on her lips. Then he slid down the straps of her gown that fell to the floor. She removed his robe. They stood facing each other. He passionately kissed her neck and other parts of her body. Suzanna's desire for him increased. He lifted her in his arms while kissing her lips fervently and laid her gently on the bed. The strength of his chest on her body stimulated her. They made passionate love for the first time and repeated it soon after. Richard's experience in lovemaking pleased her tremendously. His delicate moves and words of adoration showed his genuine love for her.

Richard was far more intense than she had ever expected. He was a great lover. Before the night ended, they opened a bottle of

Alexandra Lamour

champagne in their room and drank it while she sat on his lap on a sofa.

"I love you dearly," he began. "I did not know you were not a virgin."

Suzanna paused and told him about Edward. "I was inexperienced and fell for him quickly. I hope that does not anger you."

"No more secrets, Suzanna. I beg of you."

"I promise you, Richard. I would never want to jeopardize our love … ever." Suzanna knew the discussion would be addressed and was relieved by Richard's reaction.

Later, they walked on the promenade deck, arm in arm, and spoke about their goals and aspirations. The idea of having children someday made them happy. Their conversations seemed to never want to end, and they endlessly shared their ideas and feelings. Suzanna shared her opinion of Lady Merisel. "Richard, she has never liked me. From the first day of our arrival, I felt tension whenever she was around."

Richard grinned and said, "Merisel can be difficult to tolerate." He reassured her it was best to ignore her condescending comments.

They discussed their preferences and dislikes in jest. Suzanna mentioned her childhood fears, and Richard listened intently.

Richard said, "My biggest fear is being left alone without you. The very thought of never seeing you again—"

"Please do not talk in such a way. We should watch what we say because life can test us. Sometimes what we fear in life will come to us."

"You're not a fatalist, are you?" Richard looked out at the dark ocean. The moon's light danced on the waves.

"A little, I guess, but I'm also an optimist." She tapped her foot on the floor. "I believe that nature is in control and will put us to the test to strengthen us. If not, life would be so easy … boring. We need to face our fears and challenges without fail to become stronger, better individuals. Many events in life are for our benefit."

"My, my. You have said a mouthful," Richard remarked.

"And what makes you happiest?"

"I am looking at my greatest happiness of all." He held her in his arms. "Cold?"

"A little," Suzanna said. "Let us stay out a little longer. It is such a splendid evening. Hold me close. Don't ever let me go."

On the morning of the fourth day, the ship approached Cagliari, on the southeastern part of Sardinia. When Suzanna awoke, Richard was already dressed. She stretched her arms, yawned, and asked, "How long have you been watching me sleep?"

"Oh, for a couple of years." He chuckled. "It's time for breakfast, Lady Waterford. Would you like to eat privately or in the dining room?"

"Why, Lord Waterford, you know how much I love dining rooms. There will be so much more to feast my hungry eyes on."

She hugged him, knowing their souls were connected. When their lips met, he pulled her closer, fulfilling every need and comfort. Nothing else could bring such delight. To love one another wholeheartedly was true love's meaning. One-sided love didn't count. Aware of how ludicrous she had behaved with Edward, she dismissed the memory. It seemed to be part of another world.

He reached for her and said, "I think we better head for breakfast before it is time for lunch."

"Give me a few minutes. If you wish, I will meet you there. That way, you will be able to secure us a good table."

"Great idea." He put on his hat and left.

"I am right behind you, my darling," she said in the hallway.

"Oh good ... you got ready so quickly," he said when she reached him.

Suzanna appreciated the sandy white beaches of the island as the ship approached nearer. The sun's warmth, the Mediterranean Sea, and the cool breezes probably made Richard forget about his duties back in London. A secluded island of relaxation was what they needed. They reached the dining room as the ship was about to anchor.

The passengers were chatting as they ate. After the meal, the journey to the hotel took a little over an hour. They saw small inlets, white-roofed houses, buildings that stood out against the lucid blue waters, and several fishing boats.

"This island is captivating!" Richard pointed to the jagged mountains that bordered the coastline as far as the eye could see.

"Oh yes, I have only dreamed about faraway destinations. This island will always be our special place."

The hills and mountains were untouched by human hands. The island possessed so much peace and beauty. The Hotel Italia gave them isolation and solitude. It was positioned all alone, high up on a remote cliff.

At the main entrance, a man dashed for the carriage and said, "*Signore e Signora* Waterford, *Benvenuto.* We hope you like it here. Please have a nice stay."

The hotel was simple and picturesque. Very few guests loitered in the lobby. Most of the tourists appeared to be Italian or French.

Suzanna pulled out her Italian dictionary and attempted to converse with the hotel owner.

"*Si, si, Signora,*" he answered, clapping his hands at the concierge.

"What did you say to him?" Richard asked.

"Oh, I wanted to know if the dining room had good Italian cuisine." She grinned.

"I hope you expressed your question correctly in Italian, for our sake. It would be embarrassing if the manager asked us to vacate the premises." She admired his sarcasm.

"You love to tease me so." She laughed and hit him lightly with her handbag.

The following morning, they visited stores and bought gifts from street vendors in the village. Later, a guide took them to Romanesque cathedrals and Baroque churches. They loved the castle, Castello di Padres, and its intriguing history. It was visible from every point of the city. It had a strategic location for the protection of its citizens

The Long-Kept Secret

from invaders. Its construction was in the early thirteenth century. The castle could be reached by following a small country road, the site of the tomb of the giants, Su Monte and S'Abe, from which the windy path climbed to the fortress. It was an enchanting place to visit and a mystical journey into the past.

"I think it is time to return to the hotel," Richard said. "It has been a long day."

"Yes, I agree. My legs are tired."

Richard picked up his wife, carried her down the hill, and placed her on steadier ground.

The driver was sleeping when they reached the carriage. He rose to his feet and mumbled in Italian, which caused the couple to laugh.

"Back to the hotel," Richard said.

"Si, Signore Waterford, *immediatamente*."

Suzanna giggled. "*Immediatamente*? That's quite a lengthy word."

"The people of Sardinia are unique," Richard said.

"Yes, they are simple and kind-hearted." Suzanna admired their smiling faces. She loved how eating and resting in the middle part of the afternoon were essential habits in their culture. They were always willing to go the extra mile to help visitors find their way, knowing that the rich would always reward them well. She thought of their departure. The island's warmth and England's damp and foggy weather disappointed Suzanna. She turned to Richard and asked about returning one day.

"Someday, we will return. I can promise you that." He took her hand as they approached the hotel.

"I hope so, Richard. I have fallen in love with Italian culture."

"Not as much as I have fallen in love with you." He grinned.

"Richard, promise me our love will last forever and that nothing in this crazy world will ever tear us apart. You have to promise me to honor this request. I am afraid life's challenges and complications could destroy what we have."

When their eyes met, she knew his words were always sincere. For some reason, insecurity had arisen in her soul, forcing her to believe their love might not be able to withstand the unexpected.

Alexandra Lamour

"I promise there is no reason to fear. Nothing will ever come between us. I know the future is unforeseeable. Is it not better to be that way?" He led her to a bench by the hotel's entrance. "I was lost before I met you. I was in a world of choices and regrets. And the unexpected happened. The first time I laid eyes on you, I knew you were the one that I was searching for my whole life."

Suzanna listened intently. He had opened the window to his heart.

They spent the last evening of their honeymoon in their room. Richard ordered a seafood dinner served on the terrace. It consisted of sautéed lobster and shrimp cooked in a parmesan cream sauce. The pasta consisted of fresh parsley and different fresh herbs. The savory slice of Italian brochette with butter was Richard's favorite. After the meal, they ate a garden salad with olive oil dressing.

"Richard, this is tasty. We have to bring one of the cooks home with us."

"I am enjoying it as much as you are. English food is so bland. I will look into it when we get home."

After the servant cleared the table, the dessert tray arrived with cakes, pies, tiramisu, biscotti, ice cream, Bavarian apple torte, and cookies covered with powdered sugar.

"I'll take one of each," Suzanna said with a smile.

"I will do the same." Richard chuckled and pointed to the tiramisu.

When dessert ended, Richard had coffee and dismissed the servant. "Now I can have you all to myself." He pulled Suzanna's chair closer and held her hand. "I hope you have enjoyed our stay in Sardinia."

"But it hasn't ended yet." She kissed his enticing lips. "I'll be back soon, my love." She went to the closet and found the sheer black nightgown bought in New York before they departed for England.

Richard was still sitting on the terrace when she reappeared in the moonlight. "You have left the best for last."

"I knew you would like it."

They embraced for several minutes, and then he carried her to a luxurious bed with satin sheets. As they slowly undressed and gazed

The Long-Kept Secret

into each other's eyes, their sexual energy filled them with happiness. They were soulmates.

Suzanna could only think about Richard and her love for him. Nothing else mattered at this time. They fulfilled each other's desires; their bond was physical and spiritual. She knew that true love was an unbreakable connection of devotion and an immeasurable spiritual connection. The ecstasy caused her troubles and worries to vanish into thin air.

Chapter 29

The horses' whinnying signified that Suzanna and Richard had arrived. They were happy to be home. They exited the carriage feeling stiff and a little tired from the journey.

Richard removed his hat. "Hello, everyone. We are finally home!"

Lady Merisel walked into the hallway and smiled. "How was your trip?"

"Wonderful!" He pulled out a velvet box from his pocket. "It's a little gift from the both of us. Suzanna picked it out."

"I've noticed how much you like brooches, and I thought this one would be best." Suzanna pinned it to Lady Merisel's dress.

"It's beautiful." Lady Merisel sighed. "When will you be leaving for Rothbury?"

Richard replied, "Unfortunately, the day after tomorrow ... before the break of dawn ... but I'll be back in a week."

Suzanna grimaced. "I better go change." She went to their bedchamber, wondering what it would be like during her husband's absence. The thought of him leaving her so soon made her feel uneasy. Richard's hunting trip was an excursion that he looked forward to every year, and she didn't want to destroy the feeling of anticipation.

Richard, Lord Clarence, and Sir Wilmington always gathered for a social event at the Waterford home before going to Burnham Lodge. Lord Waterford I had always encouraged his son to have the gathering, and he immensely enjoyed the men's company.

178

The Long-Kept Secret

The following evening, when Suzanna entered the salon, a group of men surrounded Sir Wilmington at the table in the middle of the room.

Richard announced, "This is my wife, Suzanna. Sir Wilmington, I know you were unable to attend our wedding."

Sir Wilmington rushed to his feet, almost knocking over his glass, and said, "My dear Lady Waterford, it is such a pleasure to meet you."

"Nice to meet you." She sat down beside Merisel, who was playing cards with Isabella.

"Enjoy yourselves," Richard whispered. "Father looks forward to this get-together for weeks before it happens."

"I can see that." She smiled.

Suzanna found Sir Wilmington fascinating. She listened to him explaining his last hunting adventure. His story attracted everyone's attention. The men's carefree flair and adventurous style contrasted with most Englishmen. Such rare dispositions had been nurtured and guided by Sir Wilmington's deceased uncle, a bachelor for life.

Isabella whispered, "Sir Wilmington was known for his charming disposition and ability to attract affluent women ... single or married. His most recent conquest was the prominent Madame Juliet Bouchard, one of Paris' most admired women. Her family belonged to the aristocracy. Juliet's family money and intellect contributed to Sir Wilmington's obsession with her. There were rumors that they had planned to run away together, but such a plan had never materialized."

Merisel added in a low voice "Nevertheless, the mention of Juliet caused him to take leave of his senses. His passion for life did not surpass his love for Juliet."

Richard and Clarence joined the table and drank merrily as the night progressed. "It is great to get away from the everyday routines. I thank you, gentlemen, for making this a wonderful gathering."

After a while, the wine began to affect Richard's senses. Suzanna noticed lethargy in his movements and wished for the small festivity to end soon.

Clarence glanced at Suzanna, and she wondered if Richard would ever find out about his secret love for her. It was best to tell him when the time was fitting since it was a way to free herself from a secret now that they were married. Above all, she had promised him that there would never be any more secrets between them. She hoped Clarence was over her and had found a new conquest.

She speculated if Richard knew the truth, it would be devastating and would destroy their friendship. However, holding back the truth made her feel dishonest.

Clarence stared at a flickering candle, and Richard drank more wine. There was another toast to honor Sir Wilmington's return to London after living abroad for a year. Soon after, the men began leaving.

When Clarence and Richard sat alone at the card table, he announced his engagement to Miss Agatha Williams. Her family's wealth would give them both a life of luxury.

"We will marry in the spring."

"I am happy for you, Clarence. One last toast to marriage—and may it last forever."

The ladies congratulated him as well.

The heaviness lifted from Suzanna's chest. The news was remarkable. *Let the secret die on its own. Furthermore, no damage was done,* she pondered.

Lady Isabella parted when her carriage arrived, and Lady Merisel went to bed. Richard and Suzanna decided to retire since the early-morning expedition to Rothbury required a sound and alert mind.

The following morning could not have arrived any sooner. Lord Clarence's arrival was made known by heavy knocking at the main door. The sound vibrated in the hallways, waking up her father-in-law.

Richard dressed and told the servant he would be ready momentarily. He was exhausted from a lack of sleep. He left a letter for Suzanna on the table as she slept soundly, and he gently kissed her forehead.

Chapter 30

Richard had already left when Suzanna awoke from an alarming dream. She felt troubled as she got out of bed. The letter on the table lightened the dark feeling within her. It stated how deeply Richard loved her, and he said he would always keep her close to his heart despite their separation. The necklace with a golden locket containing his picture, which he had bought in Sardinia, was still around her neck.

Yawning and stretching her arms, she dressed in simple attire. She placed the folded letter in her handbag and snapped it shut. Lady Merisel was probably eating breakfast on the terrace with her father-in-law dozing at her side.

In the afternoon, Suzanna and Lady Merisel enjoyed tea and sweets on the terrace. It was a gloomy day. The morning fog was dispersing as the sun attempted to sneak out from behind the dark clouds, but the clouds did not allow its rays to shine brightly. The dreary day enhanced Suzanna's feeling of loneliness. She reflected on Richard's parting words, and she was disappointed he did not wake her before his departure.

Lady Merisel's friends appeared in the early part of the afternoon. They were only interested in gossip and their selfish desires. They spoke of the latest French fashions, Queen Victoria's daughters' marriages, and the old Duke of Norfolk, widowed and engaged to a Swedish princess thirty years his junior.

Lady Amelia, leader of the group, raised her head high and said to Suzanna, "I have heard America is not a desirable place to live. I've read there are social-level issues and racial injustices. And those wretched Native Americans are a constant concern. Is this true, Suzanna?"

Richard had already told Suzanna that Lady Amelia thrived on gossip. Unless she dismissed the facts as incorrect, her friends refused to believe anything else.

All eyes focused on Suzanna. It was one of the most heart-wrenching days of her life, and such comments were inevitable. She knew accepting Lady Merisel's request to join her friends could lead to trouble. She should have never allowed Lady Amelia to provoke her. Suzanna knew Lady Merisel would not defend her. It was her way of getting back at her for marrying her brother. Their laughter infuriated Suzanna as she thought of words that would put Lady Amelia in her place.

"Oh my, Lady Amelia, you have discovered some truths. However, I must say that social and racial issues exist in England. As for the Native Americans, they had been living in America for hundreds of years before Europeans arrived. And the mistreatment by Europeans put them in disgraceful conditions. They are fighting for survival on stolen land."

In the silence that followed, Suzanna excused herself from the gathering. Lady Amelia was speechless. She had tried her patience. She had absolutely nothing in common with Lady Merisel and her friends.

The next morning, Suzanna saw Lady Merisel in the foyer alone. "We have to talk now, Suzanna. Please follow me into the library."

Suzanna followed, feeling very uncomfortable. Something told her peril was lurking in the library.

The Long-Kept Secret

Lady Merisel closed the door and said, "When Richard returned from America to share his plans to marry an American, it struck us with grief, especially when there are so many ladies of quality to choose from here. I knew there would be trouble."

"I don't understand, Merisel. What have I done to make you so angry? Why are you telling me this now and not before our marriage?"

"Before? I received the news this morning!" She raised her voice. "God only knows why it didn't arrive before the ceremony. Take it! Look at it!"

The paper was authentic: signed, dated, and stamped by the Charleston County Courthouse. Suzanna's eyes finally stopped midway down the page: "Priscilla Connelly, an African American servant, bore a daughter named Suzanna in 1851 and died at childbirth."

"The news arrived momentarily. I knew something was wrong with you, something mysterious!" Lady Merisel held the folded letter in her quivering hand. "Poor Richard! It will kill him! I truly believe he will not be able to handle such devastating news! I will never be able to show my face in public again! Oh my, my head is pounding beyond belief!"

Suzanna was informed about her sister-in-law's performances and knew how the weaknesses of others made her feel strong. She cared very little about anyone except herself. Remorse was growing inside Suzanna as she contemplated her situation. "I swear I knew nothing of this, and if I did, I would have informed Richard." A tight knot formed in Suzanna's stomach. The family's name was now *at stake!*

"How will I break the news to my father?" she shouted. "It will surely destroy him!"

Suzanna asked one of the servants for a glass of water and fanned herself. The thought of Waterford's social circle finding out about her past caused her to panic. She rose from her seat. The letter was unbelievable. "Fuchsia told me my mother was Priscilla Hathaway, a British servant. There has to be a mistake!"

183

Alexandra Lamour

"Well, she lied to you! How can it be a mistake? Look at the mayor's signature. This letter is notarized." Lady Merisel approached Suzanna and pointed to the letter's seal with a trembling hand. Then she handed it to her.

It felt like her death warrant! The mayor's signature possibly might as well have been written in blood! *How could this be,* she contemplated? Suzanna didn't look like an African American woman. She felt and behaved like a white American woman. Her mind drifted in and out of reality. Then she looked at it again. "I don't know your intentions, but Richard loves me. He will love me through thick or thin—our love will not die!" She dropped the letter that held her fate. Feeling like an unwelcome stranger in her home, she headed toward the door.

"Suzanna, before you decide—and if you truly love him—you better leave for good. The information will destroy our family's name. And all we have ever done to keep our name honorable will have been in vain!"

Suzanna let her pride distort her thinking as she began to pack her clothes. Stopping for a moment, she looked at her hands and turned them. They looked normal, human, like everyone else's, African American or white American, a servant like her mother or a lady. *God loves us all, regardless of our origins,* she believed. In a trance, she stood before the mirror. Her eyes saw what the world saw—and maybe more.

She was from two different worlds, but it didn't matter to her. While touching her arms and legs, she forced a smile. *The truth always comes out. Oh yes, and the truth will set you free.* She thought of a sermon she had heard as a child and packed her belongings begrudgingly. Fuchsia had hidden the long-kept secret so well.

Within the hour, she had all of her baggage before her. She tried to write Richard a letter to explain everything but realized the words were too difficult to put on paper. She sighed with a stiff upper lip and prayed God would be with her. *Lady Merisel is right. It is best to leave if it is the only way to salvage their family name. How could a name have greater importance than the love of two people?*

The Long-Kept Secret

The estate didn't seem as grand as Suzanna descended the circular staircase. The walls appeared cold, made of materials that couldn't feel like her, unwelcoming, and empty. Her baggage followed her down the stairs with the help of two servants.

Midway down the staircase, Suzanna saw Lord Waterford I wheeling himself and stopping at the library doorway. He was calling Merisel's name frantically.

Suzanna gestured for the servants to place her baggage at the main door, and she sat on the hallway loveseat to listen to their conversation.

"And may I ask what that was all about?" Lord Waterford I shook his cane at Lady Merisel.

"Oh, Father, must you ask me now? Can't this wait until tomorrow? Please let me be." She tried to leave, but he grabbed her dress, jerking her back.

"From a child, you've been mischievous. Always believing the world should think like you and behave like you. God help us!" He clasped his shaking hands.

Suzanna leaned closer, listening through the partially open door.

"I'm old enough to take any news. I've seen more and heard more than you'll ever know. I've survived the deaths of my beloved wife and my third child. There is nothing you can say that would shock me. Now, Merisel, if you don't answer me at this moment, I'm going to have to bend you over my knee and spank you the way I used to when you were a naughty child." His breathing grew heavier. "You were always harder to handle than Richard ... a little like your mother."

"Father, your dear daughter-in-law, Suzanna, has disgraced us! She has mocked us!" she shouted.

"And may I ask what this angel of loveliness could have done so wrong that it has caused her to leave the library so abruptly?"

"That ... that angel of loveliness is an angel of darkness." She turned and looked out the window. "Dear Father, don't make me say this to you. Please, I can't!" She turned to face him.

Suzanna put her hand to her heart.

Alexandra Lamour

"Merisel Louisa!" he shouted. "By God, if you don't tell me at once, I swear I will make you pay for the agony you are causing me."

She tried to calm him by patting his shoulder, and she walked over to the desk. "She is a mulatto."

His expression turned to disbelief.

"Her mother was Lord Montgomery's African American servant. Don't you see the seriousness of the situation? It will destroy our family name. I will never be able to face my friends again." She placed her hands over her face, trying to gain sympathy. It was her only chance to get rid of her sister-in-law, and she had to play her part well.

Suzanna was ready to leave, but she couldn't. Instead, she kept her ears wide open for the end of the conversation.

"Did she know of this when she married Richard?" he asked.

"No, she was just as surprised as I was. I have the Charleston's mayor notarized letter in the desk drawer."

"Damn you, Merisel! You are the angel of darkness! How could you be so cruel? Sending away a young lady—a lady your brother would give his life for? Are you mad, woman? You've gotten yourself in a bind." He put his hand over his quivering mouth.

"Father, you can't talk to me like that!"

"This is just the tip of the iceberg. There are some shenanigans here, and I'm sure Isabella is part of it. This time, you have gone way too far. What in heaven's name got into your thick head? I think you want others to be unhappy like you. And you wonder why your marriage was so horrendous? I pray for your safety when Richard returns because all hell will break loose!" he hollered.

He wheeled himself to the door, coughing and calling for a servant. "A dozen servants in this house, and I can't find one! And sending such a lovely young lady away! You should be ashamed of yourself, Merisel!"

Suzanna looked at her father-in-law, but she had no words to say. She froze.

"Suzanna, I need to speak with you!"

The Long-Kept Secret

She left quickly without responding. Lady Merisel's words would haunt her for a long time. She loved her father-in-law dearly, but she had no recourse. She had convinced herself it was best to leave with unspoken words.

Before entering the carriage, she glanced up at their bedchamber window where they had shared such passion. Everything had happened so quickly, and now she had to close the chapter of her life with Richard. She had never experienced such pain in her heart before.

PART V

Chapter 31

1875

The luxury steamship with 305 passengers slowly drifted into the ocean. Suzanna leaned over the railing and watched Liverpool becoming smaller and smaller and eventually turning into a little black dot. Walking along the promenade deck, memories of their journey to London stimulated her senses, kindling a flame she had endeavored to put out as she boarded the ship. *Love will find a way, and I must be strong*, she believed. She tried to eat in the dining room, but the food was heavy, too hard to swallow, and felt trapped in her mouth. It made her feel ill; the spices aroused an unpleasant feeling that forced her to leave the table.

On the promenade deck, she wandered like a lost soul; the essence of her being was crying out for help. She held back the tears. If she wept, it would be hard to regain control.

She sat on the deck, pulled out her novel, and read until the sun sank into the ocean. It was helping greatly, taking her into another world of excitement and mystery and helping to ease her mind to forget the present. The story was moving and delightful. She smiled and wept at Jane Austen's characters forced into unfavorable situations. *Yes, it is so important to be sensible and have common sense.* She felt the main character's agony when she had to make a significant decision that affected those who loved her. If this book

Alexandra Lamour

was the only thing that would get her through heartache, then so be it. It was therapeutic.

The next day—and the day after—she followed the same routine. She sat at the same place, gazed at the endless ocean, and returned to the pages of her book. Fortunately, the weather was pleasant, unlike their trip to England, and she spent most of her time on the promenade. She tried to clear her thoughts and be optimistic about her future without Richard. Letting him go was letting go of a part of her heart that would be impossible to reclaim.

She touched her neck and realized that her locket was gone. The engraving on the exterior said, "Our Love Is Forever." She thought for a few seconds, and then it all returned to her in a flash. *It was tangled, and I left it on the night table*. She was so upset with herself. It was the last gift that Richard had given her, a gift from the heart. *There's no point blaming myself now*. She dismissed the locket from her mind and began to think about more serious issues. *If I contact the Coopers when I arrive home, will they help me get through this? They were always there for me. Mr. Cooper was a great business associate and friend. I miss Lily so much*.

In the afternoon, she noticed a group of first-cabin passengers heading for the card room. Even though she didn't have a partner, she decided to join them. In Suzanna's younger years, she had played poker, twenty-one, and euchre under the supervision of Claudette. It was one way to forget the present situation for a while.

Passengers conversed as they leaned at overcrowded tables. Many smokers sat at a table next to the porthole. The card dealer at her table spoke with a Southern accent, which made her feel at home.

The first game was twenty-one, which Suzanna won, and then she played euchre with a young woman, Sarah, who was also a Southerner. She seemed eager to play with Suzanna. Her husband discussed politics with a group of cigar-smoking men.

"Nice to meet you, Sarah," said Suzanna.

"Likewise. The man with the tall hat is my dear Frank. We were recently married. And you?"

"Married, but it's a little complicated right now."

The Long-Kept Secret

Suzanna and Emily won the first round of euchre. During round two, Suzanna excused herself and returned to the promenade. She felt uncomfortable since most of the travelers had spouses.

Threatening clouds were approaching from the west, and within an hour, the sky darkened. A bitter current chilled her to the bone. Wrapping herself in her shawl, she returned to her room, alone and fearful.

The ship became unsteady as the waves crashed against its sides. The weather put the passengers and crew into a state of unrest. The ship continued to rock violently. The roaring waves and howling wind made her fearful for her life.

A crew member knocked on her cabin door and said, "Do not panic, madame. The storm will hopefully clear up soon."

"Panic? How can I not panic?"

"Madame, this kind of weather condition is normal." He left and knocked on the next door.

Several uncomfortable hours later, the storm began to subside, giving relief to the passengers. It would take almost two weeks to reach New York Harbor. Suzanna only wanted the time to pass quickly and picked up another book.

An hour later, the ship began to sway again. But this time, the storm returned with a vengeance. It was not over. Rapid knocking on her cabin door caused Suzanna to jump.

"Madame, you must put on a life jacket immediately." The steward helped her with the long strap he tied twice around her waist.

"What is happening?"

"Captain Murray requests that all passengers wear a life jacket for safety. Stay in your room unless we sound the alarm to meet on deck."

"Oh, heavens, how many lifeboats are there?"

"Plenty for every passenger and crew member."

She pulled out a wedding picture and said, "May we make it alive … oh, dear Richard … please … be with me now."

Suzanna couldn't bear the tossing about in her room, and she went down the corridor to talk to the other passengers. A group attempted to go up a short flight of stairs, but the steward stopped them. He said it was unsafe on deck and told them to remain in their rooms. The second and third-class passengers attempted to climb the stairwell. A few crew members told them to remain calm and wait for an emergency evacuation bell if disembarking the ship was necessary.

"Everyone, listen to me!' the head steward shouted. "The ship is far safer than the lifeboats for now."

Suzanna returned to her room to vomit, believing she had influenza. She wrapped her entire body with the bedcover and leaned her aching head against the wall. Her body shook, and her forehead was wet with sweat. "God, please, spare my life and everyone on the ship. Have mercy, Lord!" She found a belt in her suitcase to tie around her waist and to a chair. She hoped it would prevent her from being thrown about the room.

Regret filled Suzanna's heart. She should have stood up to Merisel's wickedness; otherwise, she would never have been in this situation. She should have waited for Richard's return because he would have understood, as always. She wondered what he was doing at the moment.

The storm persisted for several hours, causing damage to the ship, but it remained in one piece. The vessel settled into much calmer waters. Several passengers went to the infirmary due to illnesses and injuries from being tossed around in their rooms and the corridors. One of the steam engines was inoperable by the storm. Furthermore, a young crew member was tossed off the ship during the turbulence.

By the end of the week, reality began to sink in. Suzanna created a checklist of duties that needed to be addressed. First was the bank— to find out how much money she had earned during her absence— and then was a place to live. She wanted to purchase a home in the city to be close to the factory. Her last annual bank summary—dated April 1, 1874—stated there was nearly two thousand dollars in profit. Adding the profit to the sale amount of the plantation pleased her greatly.

Just when everything seemed to be going so well from a financial perspective, her most cherished figurine from Sardinia fell from an

The Long-Kept Secret

opened baggage onto the floor and broke in half. She believed it was best to put it away since it only brought more grief. She took a deep breath and folded her arms across her chest. It was best to let go of the past and to move forward. Richard was on her mind. *Maybe he will hate me forever. Maybe he loves me.*

Her sister-in-law's devious behavior exasperated her again. She always rehearsed her lines so well. It was evident that Lady Merisel felt threatened by Suzanna and wanted her to have no association with the Waterford family. A scratchy feeling in Suzanna's throat caused her to cough, and she decided to request a physician.

Within an hour, a very old doctor appeared at her door. "My name is Dr. Lancaster." He bowed his head and led her to a seat. "Are you related to Lord Bartholomew Waterford I?" He examined her throat with a shaky hand.

"I recently married his son, Lord Richard." She kept her eyes lowered to avoid further discussion.

"My, how is the young chap?" He looked around the room. "I haven't seen him for some time. I was his mother's physician. She was quite a lady." He stopped abruptly. "Poor soul hemorrhaged to death after the stillbirth of her third child, another male. It took a long time for Bartholomew to recover. He never remarried."

"Nobody told me about this." She thought about the grief her father-in-law must have carried over the years.

The doctor said, "Were you married at St. Paul's Cathedral?"

"Yes." She hoped he would stop asking questions.

"Quite a prestigious cathedral, I must say." He took off his glasses and rubbed his eyes. "Your health needs serious care." He reached into his leather bag. "You have a mild case of croup. Take this medicine every six hours. It will prevent it from getting any worse. Bed rest and lots of fluids are mandatory. There have been several cases reported on board these past few days. Keep warm and get comfortable. I will be back tomorrow to see how you are feeling. You will probably get a slight fever. It hasn't reached its peak yet."

He refused to take her money. Then he walked toward the door.

Suzanna was relieved it was not serious.

Alexandra Lamour

"Thank you very much, Doctor. I appreciate your help." She coughed. "Will I see you in the morning?"

"I have a few patients who have critical conditions. I'll be back tomorrow afternoon. It has been a long day."

Her symptoms were becoming more apparent throughout the day. She changed into a nightgown and tried to rest. Then she reminisced about her life with Richard and drifted off to sleep.

Chapter 32

Richard arrived late in the evening from a tiresome trip—but happy to know he would be holding his wife soon. He had been thinking about Suzanna constantly and was eager to share his hunting adventures. He took the kerosene lamp in his hand, rushed up the stairs, and opened the bedchamber door. His face was gleaming with anticipation. Noticing that the bed was empty and some of Suzanna's personal belongings were absent, he called for one of the servants. "May I ask where my wife is?"

The young servant walked toward him and slipped the golden locket into his hand. "Gone, my lord. It has been a week since she left. I found the locket under the bed."

"I don't understand. Did you find anything else in the room? Did she leave a letter?" He was devastated. He paced about the room, rubbed his hands through his hair, and turned to the servant. "Thank you, Mary. You are dismissed."

"I'm so sorry, my lord. I miss her as well." She curtsied and left the room.

He paced more, clasping his hands in a prayer position. He went to Lady Merisel's room and was surprised to see her still awake. She was writing a letter at her desk, and the door was open. She turned and gasped. "You startled me half out of my wits. I didn't hear you coming,"

Richard was fuming as he approached her. "Where is Suzanna?"

Alexandra Lamour

"She didn't tell you? Was there not a note or letter in her room?"

"No, Merisel!" He squeezed the locket, and his face turned red. "There was no letter. Where is my wife? What has caused her to leave me? I don't understand what has happened. Merisel, I know you. What have you done?"

Lord Waterford I wheeled himself to the doorway and said, "Richard, my son, something awful did happen during your absence. But nothing can be so severe that it can't be mended. There is usually a solution to every problem if you search hard enough for an answer. When your mother died, I wished I could have joined her, but I had you and Merisel to keep under my care. Please sit down. Your sister— is still mischievous—and stirs up trouble."

"Father, why are you so cruel?" Lady Merisel replied.

"Silence, Merisel!" He shook his finger at her.

"Richard, your sister received information about Suzanna—."

"Father, I told you everything about her illegitimate birth. Her mother was a British servant, unmarried to her father, a lord. Why must we go through this again?"

Lord Waterford I shook his head. "There is more. Her half-sister, Fuchsia, had hidden the truth about her mother. Her mother's name was Priscilla Connelly, not Priscilla Hathaway, and she was an African American servant of Lord Montgomery."

"Are you sure of this? Is the letter authentic?" Richard asked.

Lord Waterford I took the letter from his pocket. Then he handed it to his son. "Remember, she did not take you for a fool. She knew nothing of the letter."

Richard looked at his sister and his father and paced back and forth. He saw Suzanna's face, and her eyes were calling to him. He could hear her sweet voice and see her lips moving, telling him she loved him. A burst of energy soared through him. His soul told him what to do. He had to go to her. He had to tell her it didn't matter. He had to tell her he loved her more than life and would lay down his life for her. She was an integral part of his world, and she meant everything to him. She was his beam of sunlight. When she was away, emptiness encompassed him. The intolerable darkness was

198

The Long-Kept Secret

hard to escape. Thinking about the sorrow she was probably feeling stung his heart's core. The thought of her being ill or troubled—with no one to comfort her—troubled him. No weapon or wound could cause the pain he felt for her now. There was enough time to heal the pain and accept whatever destiny awaited them. "I must go to her." He headed for the door. Nothing was going to stop him from finding Suzanna.

"Stop!" Lady Merisel shouted. "You are making a big mistake! Do you not care what others will say of us? What will become of our name?" She covered her face with her hands.

"It was you who caused this! Pray, woman, that no harm has come to her!" He quickly departed.

Lord Waterford I's eyes followed his son as he left. "Godspeed, my son."

Lady Merisel's face looked like she had seen a ghost.

Chapter 33

New York City welcomed Suzanna with open arms. She was relieved to finally place her feet on solid ground and breathe more freely. Her heart yearned to speak with the Coopers as soon as possible, and she headed for their estate. They would be shocked to see her again so soon. It was close to a year since she departed as Richard's fiancée. It all seemed like a dream now. The dream lingered in the back of her mind as she wondered. *What will they think of me? What will they think about Merisel? What advice will they give me?*

She saw fishermen bringing in their daily catch. She had once loathed the odor of fish and the salty ocean, but she now appreciated them more than ever. She was home, safe and sound, and whatever fate lay before her, she had the strength to meet its challenges. Nothing could make her fall again! Her strength moved her forward. Her strength was an insurmountable energy that had gotten her to where she was.

The weather was still warm, and there was still some time before summer would end. Mrs. Cooper's colorful plants gave Suzanna a feeling of warmth and acceptance. The immaculate gardens brought serenity to her troubled mind. Bliss filled her heart as the estate appeared before her, but she was taken by surprise when Lily opened the door.

"Oh, Lily!" She reached out for her as though she was touching part of her past. "I didn't think you would still be here."

The Long-Kept Secret

They hugged for some time.

Lily said, "Lady Waterford, we heard about your wedding. You must be so happy."

"I'm so glad you remained with the Coopers."

"I feel at home here. They have been wonderful to me."

Mrs. Cooper approached Suzanna with welcoming arms and a warm smile. "What a pleasant surprise! Where's Richard?"

Suzanna grabbed her hand as they walked to the salon. She told Mrs. Cooper everything that had happened,

Mrs. Cooper stroked Suzanna's silky hair and whispered, "All is well, my dear."

"I hope so," whispered Suzanna. "I hope I didn't behave irrationally."

Mr. Cooper walked into the salon and stated, "I would recommend a trip back home to search for some information about your mother. You must have a lot of unanswered questions. I'm sure that someone who knew your mother personally is still alive. Then you will have some closure. Understanding your past can mend your present problems. You can't move forward without closure."

Suzanna gazed at him and said, "You're right. I already feel better just thinking about it, but it will be like looking for a needle in a haystack. I don't know where to begin?"

Mrs. Cooper said, "We will do everything to help you. My dearest friend lives in Charleston, and I will send her a telegram. She can visit the orphanage first to gather as much information as possible."

"Thank you very much. You have been more like family than anything else." Suzanna yawned. "I've been feeling so tired lately. I had croup on the ship. I need to get my strength back."

"First, you need to eat something," Mrs. Cooper insisted.

"I think I will pass, but maybe later."

Mrs. Cooper turned to her husband and said, "Calvin, I find it hard to believe that Richard won't come looking for her. I know him too well. He is such a romantic, and he is so devoted to people. Once he commits, he doesn't let go."

"Do you truly believe that, Mrs. Cooper?" Suzanna asked. "My deepest prayer is that he will accept me for who I am."

"I guess you will have to be patient. Love will prevail." Mr. Cooper took his wife by the hand and patted her on the back. "And how are you feeling today?"

"Much better, I must say. I feel the medicine is helping greatly." She kissed him.

Mr. Cooper continued, "Suzanna, I will be making some contacts as well, and we will see what information we can gather. I think it would be sensible to have Lily accompany us on the trip." He led his wife to the dining room.

"Thank you, Mr. Cooper. I am happy you will be coming to Charleston!"

"Of course," he replied.

Within a week, Suzanna, Lily, and Mr. Cooper were boarding the train for Charleston. Mr. Cooper had asked the mayor to locate the workers from the plantation when Lord and Lady Montgomery were alive. A formerly enslaved man, Ervin Jacobs, claimed he knew Priscilla Connelly.

Suzanna looked at the address and was pleased to discover Ervin Jacobs lived with his wife outside of Charleston. Jacobs was old and bedridden. She prayed he still had his wits about him so that she could gather as much information as possible. Finding someone who had known her mother was a miracle.

"Lily, did you remember to pack the gifts for Mr. and Mrs. Jacobs?" Suzanna fussed with her hair and straightened the waistline of her dress.

"Yes, I packed everything this morning." Lily reached for some of the lighter packages.

Their compartment was nice and cozy, and they enjoyed each other's company.

The Long-Kept Secret

Suzanna passed Lily one of her favorite books to read. Suzanna was amazed by the clarity of Lily's pronunciation and how well she projected her voice.

Lily stopped reading and looked up at Suzanna. "I want to go to school to get a good education. I have my heart set on Oberlin College. I want to become a teacher and help people who can't read. Will you help me?"

"Most definitely … you know I will." Suzanna smiled warmly.

"There seems to be something ailing you. Your color doesn't look so good." Lily touched Suzanna's forehead.

"I was ill on the ship, and I think it took a lot out of me. I'll be fine in a few days."

She closed her eyes and had flashes of Richard. She could see his face; it was sorrowful, almost lost. It frightened her immensely. She feared he couldn't handle the news and might lose his mind. Her mind drifted back to Sardinia, the calm Mediterranean, and the warm sunlight on her body. It was so peaceful, so far away from the rest of the world, private and romantic. Suzanna's heart yearned for him. He was so far out of reach, yet she felt like she could almost touch him when she closed her eyes. Her soul called out to him in despair.

Chapter 34

When they arrived in Charleston, Suzanna recognized the road that led to the plantation. A force of vitality overpowered her. As she dismounted the carriage, optimism filled her heart.

Lily and Suzanna shared a hotel room, and Mr. Cooper stayed across the hall. Suzanna asked Lily to join her as the driver drove them around the city. Bittersweet memories of the past seemed so long ago filled her mind. Mr. Cooper stayed in his room to rest.

The warm weather helped lift Suzanna's mood. Most things had stayed the same since they had left the city. At Maurice's shop, Margaret was assisting a lady with a wedding dress. Mr. Ferrel's Mercantile Store was busy, and people entered and exited swiftly.

The driver drove by Edward's residence as a young couple with two small girls was leaving the house. The man was locking the door. Edward must have sold his home and moved to the North. They passed the library and left the city.

Suzanna had traveled that way many times. The road was a little bumpy, making her feel nauseous again. "How strange, Lily. I've never felt ill during travel."

"Mam, it's important to make an appointment with Dr. Bridge when we return to the hotel."

"Yes, I think you are right. Something strange is happening to me, and I feel a little queasy." Suzanna leaned her head out of the

204

carriage and vomited. "Maybe it was something I ate. I'm glad we are postponing the trip to the Jacobs until tomorrow."

Lily said, "We should return to the hotel. We can visit other places when you are feeling better." She wiped Suzanna's brow with a handkerchief. "I don't mean to be outspoken, but I think you are with child. You need to visit the doctor as soon as possible."

"Oh my, Lily! You could be right. I'll be sure to visit Dr. Bridge's office—after our trip to Ervin Jacobs' house."

In the morning, Suzanna and Lily headed out without Mr. Cooper. Ervin Jacobs lived in a shack a couple of miles outside of Charleston.

Even though Suzanna was not feeling well, she would not cancel the trip. It could free her from her heartache. "We must continue. We can't turn back. We traveled so far," she declared.

The poorly maintained shack stood on a bare piece of land. There was a small garden in front of the dwelling. To the side of the house was a rickety old wagon. A tiny woman with grayish-white hair tucked under a bonnet greeted them. She was smiling and missing teeth. "Mighty fine to meet yaw ladies." She wiped her hands on her torn apron and shook their hands as they exited the carriage. Her fingers were short and plump, and she held a tight grip. "We was expectin' yaw folks yesterday. That's OK. Now come on in. I've got some hot apple pie. I hope yaw all like it."

"Oh, thank you, ma'am," Lily said. "It smells just like Mama's."

Lily sat down and devoured her piece of pie and then asked for a second helping. She commented about how delicious it was and asked for the recipe.

Suzanna drank water from the well and tried to cool her burning body with a fan.

"What's ailin' you?" Mrs. Jacobs touched Suzanna's forehead.

"I'm not sure. Can we see your husband?"

Alexandra Lamour

"Let me go in and spy on him." She giggled. "I said those fine-lookin' ladies of great wealth are here to see yaw. Ervin, did yaw hear me?" She peeked around the curtain. "He's partially deaf. Yaw got to holler—or he just doesn't hear yaw."

Suzanna went in alone and sat on the rocking chair by the window.

Ervin jumped up from the bed and scrutinized her face. He was way over six feet tall. His voice was frail and low-key. "My, my, you sure look like Priscilla. I knew your ma when she was just a little gal. She was such a pretty little thing with beautiful light copper skin." He shook his head to the right and then to the left side.

"Oh, tell me, please. What was she like?" Suzanna's eyes filled with wonderment.

"She was a lively young gal with high hopes and dreams. And when she went to work for the Montgomery family with her sister, Georgette, she was so happy. They was treatin' her so well. I worked out in the fields, but Priscilla was a servant to the lady of the house. They had her dressed in fine clothes, and her hair was lookin' all fancy. I think she even learned how to read. Always gigglin' and wantin' to help others." He blew his nose. "Everyone was jealous of how well Priscilla was treated. We used to see her goin' places with the lady of the house. They went everywhere together. And when Lady Montgomery was with child, she was always by her side, tryin' to make sure that she was well taken care of … the same way they took good care of her." He rubbed his beard.

Suzanna's eyes widened. "Don't stop—please tell me more."

"Well, the last thing I recall was the lady of the house was mighty angry about somethin' and sent her away. We didn't know what happened since we never saw her again."

He spat into a bowl on the table and then released a horrendous cough. Suzanna's eyes filled with tears.

"But then, a few days later, Georgette came back with the sad news about your ma's death. It nearly broke your auntie's heart. She cried for days. Lady Montgomery had already felt so bad about sendin' her away, and when she heard that Priscilla died after delivering a girl, it almost broke her heart too. She took pity on Georgette and

The Long-Kept Secret

brought her into the house to work. And she became very close to Lady Montgomery. She raised your half-sister, Fuchsia, like she was her own. She loved her so much. I guess she used to pretend it was yaw." He pointed at Suzanna.

Suzanna shed tears of relief. At first, it had caused deep pain in her heart, but now the long-kept secret, hidden for so long, was fully explained. She dried her teary eyes, took a deep breath, and exhaled slowly. She held her handkerchief against her mouth, and her shoulders relaxed. She clasped her moist hands together, and a feeling of consolation took over. Amazingly, after so many years, finally hearing the truth was comforting. She looked about the simple room that filled her heart with peace. Her mother was raised in a similar home before she moved to the plantation. She felt at ease in such a humble environment, and Mr. and Mrs. Jacobs' kindness moved her.

The news wasn't as bad as she had anticipated. It wasn't the end of the world. The timing appeared perfect since the information was now much easier to accept. She rose and kissed his brow. Then she thanked him for taking the time to share her mother's life. She felt the kiss was symbolic of coming to terms with her past. It healed the agonizing wounds that crept up periodically.

He added, "I'm so sorry, child. If yaw had met your mother, yaw would have loved her. Take that thought with yaw. She was a rare beauty, just like yaw. Everyone who met Priscilla couldn't help but love her. I didn't mean to cause yaw so much grief. Sometimes the truth hurts so badly, but yaw know the truth always makes us feel better. It is a healing process, and no doctor can heal you like God Almighty." Then he added, "As for your father, he was never the same when she disappeared from the plantation. He always had a look of heartache."

It seemed like her parents truly loved each other, which was comforting. She wanted to tell him she was fine but did not. His fatigue was considerable. Instead, she patted his arm gingerly and thanked him. He was the last link, a living connection to her mother. She lifted the curtain and went back to the kitchen.

"Thank you." She sighed. Then they shook hands.

"My, yaw sure is a lady, wearing such fine clothes and all. So nice to meeting y'all."

Suzanna gave her the gifts and a pouch full of money.

The woman's eyes lit up, and she thanked her many times. Mrs. Jacobs stood by the door as the carriage left.

There was little conversation during their trip back to the city—until Suzanna asked the driver to take her to Dr. Bridge's clinic. She was fortunate to be the last patient.

He led her into the examination room.

After half an hour, Suzanna excited the room with her hands over her mouth.

Lily grabbed her arm and whispered, "What is it?"

Suzanna whispered, "I'm with child. What am I going to do?"

"Don't you worry now. Everything will be OK."

"Raising a child without a husband is my deepest concern. I will be looked at with contempt."

When they returned to the hotel, Suzanna sat down with Mr. Cooper. "I am with child. The thought of raising a child without a father is devastating."

Mr. Cooper sat back in his chair. "I see. My dear, there are some consequences for deserting your husband. I understand why you fled, but be aware of what you could endure for such an action, especially if Richard's family encourages him to divorce you."

Suzanna covered her face with her hands and began to cry. A divorce was the last thing she wanted. She felt herself tumbling downward and spiraling into a web of confusion and desolation. Emotional agony overcame her. "I will face the consequences. I

The Long-Kept Secret

know divorce is condoned in England for the wealthy and is much easier today."

"Let's hope Richard has no intention of requesting one since you and your child will lose whatever financial assets you could inherit. The canned food business is profitable and will keep you both comfortable. I foresee even greater growth. If this does happen, you and your child will never be needy.

Suzanna did not want to discuss the topic any further since it made her head ache terribly. She was aware of societal scrutiny and the significant consequences if he decided to divorce her. She fought her weaknesses and forced herself to be stronger. Her love for Richard grew even more as time passed. Longing for him became her constant companion.

The following morning, Suzanna's throat was scratchy and dry. She had hardly slept all night, thinking about what to do next. The first thing on her mind was adding her mother's name to the tombstone. She got out of bed and looked out the window. A mixture of sounds of the horses and wagons passing by penetrated her ears. Everyone was absorbed in their daily routines. Nostalgia for Richard overcame her, and she felt deserted and alone.

Suzanna got dressed, brushed her hair, and sat in front of the dresser mirror. She was going to be a mother soon, and that would bring many responsibilities. Regardless of everything that happened, she was going to make sure that her child was taken care of—from the best schools to the finest clothes—and would never know hunger. *My child will never feel the childhood neglect that I encountered— not as long as I'm alive,* she pondered.

A knock at the door broke her train of thought.

Lily wore her finest cotton dress and hat with lace around the rim. "I need to visit my folks before we leave. I am going to spend the day with them."

"Of course." Suzanna smiled. "Don't worry. We probably won't be leaving until the day after tomorrow. I need to visit the plantation today."

"Did you want me to go with you?"

Alexandra Lamour

"No. I need to go alone."

Lily fidgeted with her hat and left quietly.

A rustling sound in the hallway got Suzanna's attention, but she continued putting her belongings in her handbag. She thought about a hearty breakfast in the dining room. Remembering Dr. Bridge's advice about the importance of lots of sleep and regular meals, she opened the door.

Her hand touched something odd. Her expression changed to confusion when she saw the golden locket dangling over the doorknob. It was her necklace. *How did it get there? How is that possible? Could it be Richard? Did he follow me to Charleston?* She felt a presence behind her and jerked her body around.

Richard stood before her. He was smiling.

She reached for his body and wrapped her arms around him. They were comforted in each other's arms. "Richard! I'm so glad to see you! I've missed you so much!"

Smothering her face with kisses, he pulled her closer. His eyes reflected comfort, love, and strength.

"I've dreamed of this reunion for weeks." He rocked her in his arms. "I would have gone to the ends of the earth to find you. Nothing was going to stop me!"

Suzanna's eyes twinkled, and all the apprehension and loneliness were swept away in an instant. Even the knot in her stomach that she had for so many weeks disappeared.

"Everything is going to be fine," he whispered. "The past doesn't matter. I've told you this before. Please believe me." He held her tightly and caressed her hair.

"Let's sit down in the salon. There is so much I need to tell you." She placed her hand on his shoulder.

Mr. Cooper knocked on the door, awestruck when he saw Richard. "Richard, I'm so glad you made the right decision and came to Charleston."

"Charlotte gave me all the information, and I took the next train." Richard shook Mr. Cooper's hand and sat beside Suzanna. "Have you decided to move here?"

The Long-Kept Secret

"No, we will be returning to New York soon. Mr. Cooper decided it would be best to get some questions answered about my mother. He located Mr. Jacobs, and he knew her quite well."

"Well, I will leave you two lovebirds alone." Mr. Cooper smiled and left.

Richard had so many things to share with Suzanna. Holding her tightly in his arms warmed his blood. They would find a place of their own once they returned to England, and he would build a beautiful home surrounded by gardens. He would do anything under the sun to make her forget the past. Everything would turn out fine. No one would ever hurt her again for as long as he lived.

She declared, "I am with child, Richard!"

Richard's face filled with cheerfulness. "I will be a father? I couldn't be happier, my darling." Sharing the joy of a child with his wife filled his heart with bliss.

"The visit truly healed me. Mr. Jacobs knew my mother. He shared some wonderful things about her."

He reached for her hand. "I'm sorry I wasn't with you." He hugged her again, moving his hand down to her golden curls. "I can't express how much I missed you. My life means nothing without you."

"I feel the same way." She kissed his lips tenderly. "There is something I have to do. I need to go back to the plantation. I need to say goodbye. Something is drawing me there, Richard. I have to go tomorrow … alone."

"Then, you shall go, but you must at least have a driver." He held her tightly in his arms. "You silly goose." He chuckled. "You had me scared to death."

Leaving for the plantation in the afternoon meant she would return before dusk. Suzanna's heart stirred as they drew nearer. When she arrived at the graves, she was happy to see her mother's name on the tombstone. "Now you will have recognition, my dear mother," she whispered. She read her family members' names: "Priscilla and Georgette Connelly, Jonathan and Elizabeth Montgomery, and— last but not least—Fuchsia O'Reilly." She leaned over and touched Fuchsia's engraved letters. The mysterious inscription appeared to

Alexandra Lamour

be life-giving. She knew how important it was to come back. All the gaps and loose ends fell into place. Life seemed to be so clear and understandable now. It took on new meaning!

As she continued to caress the letters, tears of insight and homesickness filled her eyes. This woman had loved her unconditionally. She was the key to life's meaning, a beacon of light, and a spiritual guide. "Thank you, Fuchsia. You always protected me." She wiped the tears of repentance from her cheeks.

As she stood over the tombstone, serenity quenched her soul. Taking one last glance at it, she realized life was about more than living and dying. It was about change and growth. And it was about love and forgiveness.

Suzanna walked toward the carriage with her head held high and grasped the skirts in her hand. Richard was on her mind—and their child—and she thanked God for allowing so much happiness in her life.

The driver assisted her as she mounted the carriage. With a sharp whistle, he shook the horses' reins and headed back to the city. The day was ending, and the sun grew dim in the distance. The sky took on various shades of gray. She glanced at the full moon rising above the faded hill, and she knew that a transformation had taken place deep within her soul. She finally felt complete. Everything had miraculously become new again.

Printed in the USA
CPSIA information can be obtained
at www.ICGtesting.com
LVHW040557081123
762972LV00003B/44